Gangsters Goons and Raving Loons

(And A Town That's Full Of Them)

By Billy Graham

Copyright © Zaffire Books

All rights reserved

The moral right of Billy Graham to be identified as the author of this book has been asserted by him in accordance with the Copyright, Designs and Patents Act 1988

No parts of this book may be reproduced or transmitted in any form or by any means without permission from the publisher. Extracts have been reproduced with the kind permission of Crestwell Publishing

Preface

During a discussion at school about what parents did for a living the teacher asked one boy what his dad's job was and the lad said, "My Dad runs the local fire station. He's the station officer." The teacher said, "That's excellent Simon. Your Dad's got a very responsible job." The teacher then asked the boy sat next to him what his dad did and the boy said, "My dad drives an ambulance. He's in charge of the local ambulance service." And the teacher said, "That's fantastic Bobby. Well done." The teacher then asked another boy what his dad did and the boy replied, "My dad runs the local prison." And the teacher said, "Excellent, Johnny! Is he the prison governor?" And Johnny said, "No Miss - he's the hardest cunt in there!"

When I first heard that joke it made me laugh - like it's probably made *you* laugh! And not only did it make me laugh when I heard it, it also brought back a memory of someone who I met whilst I was in prison over thirty five years ago.

Then a couple of years ago I read a book about Stockport that Dave Courtney wrote the foreword for and there was a story in it about one of the author's friends who was a 'gangster' – the same person who I met, and got to know, in prison. The stories also featured in a follow up book that the author did that was subsequently discontinued and banned after the author was arrested for publishing a story about illegal immigrants (wonder if two-tier Keir had anything to do with that?)

I've always fancied writing a book so I got in touch with the publisher and asked could I reproduce stories from the books and they kindly said that I could.

I ended up living in Stockport myself for a while and got to know several of those mentioned in the books. Stockport is one of the best places I've ever lived in. It's one of the rummest places I've ever lived in too!

Billy Graham.

Foreword

(From the book mentioned in preface)

I've met a few gangsters and hardmen in my time – I've been good mates with most of them! And I love having a laugh and a joke. I've also been known to play the odd prank or two. So you could say this book is right up my street. And after reading it two things came to mind. One was that Nick probably hasn't done much to boost tourism for his home town of Stockport and the other was thank fuck my street *isn't in* Stockport!

Something else that came to mind after reading it was that it reminded me of the film Lock Stock and Two Smoking Barrels. (Not a lot of people know this but the character Vinnie Jones played in the film was based on me and the scene where he smashed the sunbed canopy down on the bloke lying underneath it was something I once did.) That film had the lot. It had hardmen in it. It had gangsters in it. It had violence in it and it was funny from beginning to end. All of which made it a great film. Likewise, this book has the lot too and which is why it's a great book. Though the Stockport tourist board may not agree!

'Stop the Ride" was the title of my first book. Well now another ride is about to begin. So hold on to your hats, your sides, your wigs and your cocks (you'll find out why you'll need to keep a tight hold of them in the part about 'cottaging') and get ready for a roller coaster ride with Nick down memory lane. Well, down the A6 to be precise!

Dave Courtney

(R.I.P)

As Mad As A Hatter

If you follow football, depending on what division your team is in, you may know that Stockport County's nickname is 'The Hatters.' They got the nickname due to the fact that in the 18th century Stockport was famous for its hatting industry, exporting in excess of six million hats a year. And a lot of people who live there are mad as hatters too!

As towns and cities go Stockport probably isn't any different than any other town in England. There are plenty of places to visit and there are plenty of things to do, like there are in most towns, but there are no major tourist attractions as such. Similarly, like other towns, it has its characters and like anywhere else it also has its fair share of crime. There's even been the odd murder or two. Or three. Or four. Or five. Or six!

And it might come as a surprise to you, then again it might not, that in 2006 Stockport made it into the top ten most dangerous towns and cities in England to live based on statistics for violent assaults, drug dealing, murder, muggings and burglary. And in 2016 it was listed as being one of the most likely places in the UK to become a victim of crime.

So with Stockport not being much different to any other town in England, coupled with it not being a major tourist attraction, and add to that we've topped the crime charts once or twice, then it's understandable why perhaps Stockport isn't on most people's bucket list of places to visit before they die. However even though it's understandable why not many people would want to rush to visit here, what was less understandable was why in 1983 an internationally acclaimed singer like Frankie Vaughan would want to make a record about our town.

It was called 'Stockport', and people, not just those from around here but those from other parts of the country too, were slightly bemused as to why he'd made it. And they were even more bemused by some of the lyrics he sang, such as, "I'm going back to Stockport, it's the place for me." And they were completely baffled why he said that there was "nowhere finer" and that he "wouldn't budge from Stockport for all the tea in China." Ironically, right now, in the middle of lockdown like we are, thanks to China we can't budge out of our fucking houses let alone budge from Stockport! And forget tea, you wouldn't budge for anything *at all* from China at the moment after what those cunt's have just given us!

Quite a lot has happened over the years since that song was recorded and times have changed somewhat and if Frankie Vaughan was still alive today and he was to re-record that song now having seen the aforementioned crime statistics beforehand he may well change the line from, "I'm going back to Stockport" to "Fuck that, I'm never stepping foot in that town ever again!" And with local newspaper headlines over the years reading things like 'Notorious Gangster Shot Dead', 'Headless Body Found On Hillgate' and 'Man In Hospital After Vicious Axe Attack' then you couldn't really blame Frankie, or anyone else for that matter, for not wanting to step foot in the town.

It mystified a lot of people why Frankie Vaughan had recorded it and nobody really knew the reason why. Nobody really cared actually! Some thought he was just taking the piss. Others thought it was some kind of wind up. And some people jokingly suggested that he must have been threatened that he'd be shot if he didn't record it, and a few said he must have been on drugs. And even though those suggestions were said in jest seeing how threatening behaviour, drug dealing and people getting shot is quite common in Stockport I suppose it's feasible that any one of those explanations was the reason why he recorded it!

But the truth is the song came about after the Daily Mail ran a competition to see who could come up with the best song about Stockport. And the reason they ran the competition was because the previous month they'd printed some non too complimentary remarks about the town that didn't go down well with their readers, who, after reading that 'the best thing about Stockport is the road out' complained to the newspaper.

It wasn't just people from Stockport that complained either. Apparently people from all over the country complained. I'm not sure why they complained actually. I think a lot of the inhabitants of Stockport itself sometimes think that the best thing about it is the road out! And it could just be coincidence but have you ever noticed that the roads leading out of Stockport do tend to be far busier than the roads leading in! And it's the same with the trains. Whenever one pulls into Edgeley station far more people tend to get on it than get off! They even give warnings these days to passengers as the train pulls in. I was once coming back from London and as we approached Milton Keynes the guard announced, "The next station is Milton Keynes. Get off here if you want to get a train to Bletchley, Oxford or Aylesbury." And as we approached Edgeley he said, "The next station is Stockport. Get off here if you want to get beaten up, mugged, shot, stabbed, scammed or have your fucking head cut off!"

Obviously I made that bit up. He said 'if you're extremely desperate' not have your head cut off!

I've never thought about leaving Stockport myself by the way. But then again I live in the upmarket part - the 'quaint village' of Reddish! We'll come to that in a bit.

So in an attempt to pacify the complainants the Daily Mail ran a competition to see who could write the best song about Stockport with a prize for the winner. And guess what the first prize was? A weekend in Stockport! And the runner up got a weekend in Paris!

Judging by the prizes on offer even if Frankie Vaughan wasn't taking the piss when he recorded that song, the Daily Mail obviously were. It must be the only competition ever where the runner up was happier than the winner!

It was surprising that anyone entered the competition at all actually knowing what the prize was but over a hundred and sixty people did enter and the winner was a song writer from London called Geoff Morrow who had only briefly visited Stockport once before and when he was told that he had won he said, "I'm thrilled to have won as it means I can go back. Stockport is the kind of town that lingers in your memory - and haunts you!

Apparently Geoff Morrow had written songs for Elvis Presley, Barry Manilow and Cliff Richard and he was also friends Frankie Vaughan, who he asked to sing it, and he agreed, and that's how the song came about. And although it was unusual for a famous singer like Frankie Vaughan to record a song about Stockport it wasn't unusual for famous singers to record songs in Stockport.

Strawberry studios on Waterloo Road on Hillgate had many famous artists record there over the years including Paul McCartney, Neil Sedaka, 10cc, The Stone Roses, Mick Hucknall and Simply Red, The Syd Lawrence Orchestra, Kim Wilde, The Bay City Rollers, The Buzzcocks, New Order, The Smiths and many more.

One other famous singer to come to Stockport, although he didn't ever record any of his songs at Strawberry Studios, was David Bowie. He appeared at another well known venue in the town, The Poco A Poco nightclub, in 1970. And so the story goes that after performing there he missed the last train home to London and had to kip on a bench at Edgeley Station.

Rock 'n' Roll!

It was also rumoured that he had his wallet nicked whilst he was asleep! I can well believe that. It is Stockport after all!

The 'Poco' as it was known was situated where the Hinds Head pub is now just off Manchester Road in Heaton Chapel. It featured some of the biggest stars of the time -

although it was actually built as a cinema come ballroom - and it opened as The Empress in 1939 but two decades later in 1959 the cinema closed due to financial difficulties but the ballroom remained open under the name The Empress Cabaret Club. In 1967 the club was badly damaged by a fire and it had to close but after being refurbished it re-opened a year later as a nightclub and casino called the Poco A Poco which was a Spanish phrase.

Its reputation across the North West soon grew and it hosted a series of events featuring some of the biggest names in show business. In 1969 comedian Frankie Howard recorded a TV show there and acts like Bill Hayley and the Comets, Billy Fury and Karl Denver often did week-long residences there drawing in the crowds which flocked from other towns and cities across the North West.

It gained a reputation as the place to be and as the place to go to for a good night out but like all nightclubs it attracted those who were looking for trouble. (People looking for trouble in Stockport? Never!)

So to ensure a good night was had by all and to keep the trouble makers at bay the club employed doormen and one of the doormen that worked there had a reputation as big as the club itself, a man called Joe Walsh. Another hard man also worked there, Dennis Cotterill. I never met Joe Walsh but I remember Dennis. David Bowie should've asked Dennis to accompany him to Edgeley station that night and got him to sit with him whilst he waited for his train, and if he had have done he would have still had his wallet when he woke up in the morning.

And that's because no fucker would have dared to have swiped it if Dennis had been sat next to him!

Joe Walsh was highly respected and he had a fearsome reputation. He was 'old school' and if you were right by him he was right by you but woe betide if you stepped out of line. His reputation was such that he was often called upon by the Quality Street Gang, or the 'QSG' as they were known who ran Manchester back in the 60's, 70's and early 80's and if they had any problems that needed sorting out they'd give Joe Walsh a call.

One occasion they called upon him was when 'Jimmy The Weed', Jimmy Donnelly, had a bit of trouble at a club he owned called Nito's which was next to Stockport County's ground. It was slightly more than a 'bit of trouble' it was an attempt on his life.

As Jimmy put in his book, some of the locals in Stockport didn't like the fact he had Manchester doormen on the club and they didn't give a fuck what their reputations were; they weren't welcome in Stockport. And one night as he was driving away from the club bullets were fired at him through his windscreen but they missed. The car he was driving was left-hand drive and they'd fired at the right. His brother, Arthur, then had paint thrown over his car. Things were getting out of hand and so Jimmy rang his pal Alan Kay who ran the Poco who in turn sent Joe Walsh down - and Jimmy and Arthur had no more problems.

Just to digress for a moment, as this kind of ties in with something I get to later, just like I never met Joe Walsh (I was only a young kid when he was around) I haven't met anyone from the Quality Street Gang either though I did once get 'a look' off one of them.

A few of us were in Manchester one afternoon. I was with Grant and Trevor Jones, two brothers who were mates of mine from Offerton in Stockport. Their dad was called Tom, Tom Jones. Not that it's got anything to do with this story I just thought I'd tell you that their dad was called Tom Jones! I often do that, drift off from the story I'm telling. 'It's not unusual' for me to do it!

Shit joke. Let's move on. (Tom Jones fans will get it.)

We went in this pub. I forget where it was. It was over thirty years ago now. But I think it was at the top of Oldham Street near Ancoats somewhere. We were being a bit boisterous. Well I was anyway. That wasn't unusual either!

We bounded in there and I remember seeing this group of blokes sitting at a table across the room. They were older than us, we were only in our early twenties and they looked like they were in their mid to late forties. And because we were being a bit - or rather, *a lot* - loud, they looked over and one of them gave us a look, the kind of look that said 'pipe down.'

He held his stare on *me*. He looked at me for about five seconds. He then turned and carried on talking to his friends. He had something about him that said 'you don't want to mess with me.'

So we got served, and as the bloke behind the bar gave Trevor his change he quietly said to us, "Just have the one eh lads, and be on your way." So we did. And when we went in the next pub a bit further up the road, a little while later some guy who had been stood at the bar in the previous pub came in and we ended up chatting to him and he said that we did the right thing leaving because those blokes were the 'QSG' and the one that stared at me was Jimmy Swords.

Jimmy Swords was the hardman or 'muscle' of the Quality Street Gang and it was said that he once made it his mission to take on every other hardman, bouncer or boxer in Manchester who had a reputation, though the look he gave me was enough to get his message across (if only someone else who I became good mates with had taken a similar approach to get his message across he may well have lived longer than he did.)

Mind you, even though I've never met Arthur Donnelley or any of the Quality Street Gang personally, I do know that there was once a photo of Arthur's grandson with Barack Obama on his daughter's mantel piece - and it certainly fooled me! If you happen to be reading Arthur and you're wondering how I know, don't worry, I haven't burgled your daughter's house and I'm not a night prowler or a Peeping Tom either! I'm sure a certain person ('Mr A' from Stockport) will explain all mate.

Meanwhile, back at the Poco.

As well as all the top acts playing there and having the top doorman too, Joe Walsh, The Poco also had the top compare, the best there was, Vince Miller.

Vince is the dad of Danny Miller who plays Aaron in the television soap Emmerdale and he was known as 'Mr

Manchester' in nightclub circles. He was initially headhunted to become the compare at the Poco by the ex Manchester City footballer Keith Marsden who ran the club in the early 1960's and he was the compare there throughout.

One of the top acts booked to play at the Poco were The Real Thing who had the hit You To Me Are Everything but they never made it onto the stage that particular night.

They insisted that all the lights be turned off so that the club was in total darkness before they went on stage and then when they got on stage to turn the lights on. They told Vince that this had to be done and so Vince went and spoke to the management who said no, the lights had to remain on at all times because it was a health and safety issue. So Vince went back to their dressing room and told them. But *they also* said no, the lights had to be off. So off Vince goes again back to the management, but again they said no, the lights had to stay on.

Vince goes back and tells the group this and they weren't happy and they said that unless the lights were off they wouldn't go on stage.

Vince is now thinking, "What the fuck am I going to do?" He's got hundreds in the audience waiting for the Real Thing to go on stage but he can't introduce them because they won't budge from their dressing room unless the lights are off. So he goes up to Joe Walsh and the other doormen and tells them what the holdup is and Joe Walsh says, "They're refusing to go on stage are they? We'll see about that," and he marches down to their dressing room.

Now The Real Thing were only the real thing by name. Joe Walsh on the other hand REALLY WAS the real thing and if he told you that you were going on stage then you were going on stage! But things didn't quite go according to plan and when he went in their dressing room a big row started and during the row Joe kicked their drum and his foot went straight through it and it got stuck! A massive ruck then started and Joe ended up throwing them all out – with a big base drum stuck to his foot!

Vince said it was comical watching Joe hobbling around with a drum stuck to his leg throwing one of Britain's top acts out of the club! The only problem was Vince really was fucked now because he had no act to introduce! So he had to get his thinking cap on. And so he rang his pal Bernard Manning who said that he could get there for half ten after he'd finished his stint at his own club. So Vince got on stage and told the audience that the Real Thing had broken down on the motorway and wouldn't be appearing but that Bernard Manning was appearing instead.

Personally, out of the two, I think I'd much rather see Bernard Manning!

Vince's quick thinking saved the night. There probably weren't many people who could've got Bernard Manning, who was the king of comedy at the time, to appear at two hours notice. But that's why Vince Miller was known as 'Mr Manchester', because of his popularity and the people he knew.

Someone who knows Vince very well and who's a good mate of his is Barry McConnell, and Barry told me a story about Vince that I thought was hilarious.

Barry was in the Poco one night and he was on the balcony looking down on the stage. Barry was with his dad 'Mr Mac' (his dad was a really nice bloke, and well respected too) and they were stood next to Vince. It got to midnight and Barry said to Vince, "Are we having a top of the bill tonight?" and Vince said, "Oh shit! I forgot to introduce them."

The top of the bill was a band called Pinkerton's Assorted Colours and they'd just had a hit record and the club was packed with people who'd come to see them. They were already on stage and because Vince didn't have enough time to get down to the stage to introduce them he did the announcement from the balcony where he was stood using his radio microphone and said, "Ladies and gentlemen please welcome your main act for the evening, Pinkerton's Assorted Colours," and then turned to carry on talking with Barry and his dad, and Barry said to him, "Are they any good these?" And Vince, not realising that his microphone was still on said, "No. They're fucking shit!" His words echoed around the club and about a thousand people in there heard what he said - including the band! As Barry said, it was priceless.

I'm guessing the band didn't perform an encore that night!

The Poco A Poco was synonymous with Stockport but it finally shut its doors in the early 1980's although it did re-open again as Chester's nightclub for a few years before that closed too in around 1987. The literal translation of Poco A Poco from Spanish to English is 'little by little' and Little by Little was the title of the song Dusty Springfield was dominating the charts with when she visited the club in 1966. And little did anyone know then that in years to come the name Little would become synonymous with Stockport once again and the domination that came with it would be like nothing the town had ever seen before.

"I'm thirty now and I want to live until I'm thirty one" Chris Little once said in an interview with the Stockport Express. And he did - just. And a few months after giving that interview, and just two days after his 31st birthday, he was shot dead.

It was without doubt a shock when it happened but at the same time it probably came as no surprise to many.

Chris Little's murder was brutal and ruthless and in a way it mirrored the latter years of his life as he too could be brutal and ruthless, and it'd be fair to say that the majority of Stockport didn't shed many tears upon hearing the news of his death. A lot probably breathed a sigh of relief. It was even said that in some parts of the town they had street parties in celebration and that T shirts were printed mocking him such was the relief he was gone.

In the aftermath of his death much was said and written about him both in the local and national newspapers. Some of the stories were true, some were myth and some were lies deliberately engineered by the media. One such story very nearly resulted in the offices of the Stockport Express, which were located on Wood Street at the time just up the road from Master's Snooker Club, being burnt to the ground.

The general consensus was that Chris had it coming and that he deserved what he got. He wasn't top of most people's Christmas card list that's for sure. Just the very mention of his name used to strike fear into people. Even now, over a quarter of a century after his death his name still evokes memories and people have stories to tell about encounters with him or what they witnessed him do, and depending on whom you listen to and their association with him opinions of him will differ.

Most would say that he was a bully and when you hear of some of the things he did you'd be hard pressed to disagree with them. Even those who knew him well would agree that he didn't have to mete out some of the punishment that he did, though sometimes it was necessary bearing in mind the 'business' he was involved in, i.e. the drug business. That world is a very dangerous one and violence goes hand in hand with it and there are no rules as to when, why or to whom, or in what form punishment is dished out. So to a degree when he dished it out under those circumstances you could argue that he was within reason to do so. It was also sometimes necessary to dish it out when he was working on the doors. However a lot of the time a look, or rather a glare off him would have been enough.

He had an aura about him, a certain look that hard men have. And he could give a look, like the look Jimmy Swords gave me, that when he gave it you knew he was saying 'don't fuck with me.' He was capable of scaring the living daylights out of someone just by glancing at them. And having that kind of persona meant that he didn't really have to dish it out as much as he did. Nonetheless he did dish it out and if you were ever on the receiving end of one if his left hooks and had your jaw broken - of which there were many - or he set is Rottweiler on you, or you suffered anything similar, then nothing is going to change your view that he *was* a bully and no-one can really argue with you. But even though I can see why people said he was a bully it's a bit of a contradictory to call him one because he wasn't a bully in the true sense of the word because a bully will only pick on someone who he knows he can beat or pick on those he knows won't fight back and that certainly didn't apply to Chris. He didn't care less *who* he fought. He'd have had a fight with anybody and he didn't care how hard or how handy they were supposed to be. And he didn't care how many there was of them either.

He rarely had a 'fight' at all - a fight as in two blokes throwing punches at each other and rolling around on the floor - because more often than not only one punch was thrown, by Chris. And nine times out of ten it resulted in the person on the receiving end of it being knocked out. So even though he dished it out to people that he didn't really need to dish it out to and who he knew he could beat with one arm tied behind his back, whilst stood on one leg, he wasn't a 'bully' bully if that makes sense.

For instance, if someone said to a bully, "There's a right big handy cunt looking for you down the road and he wants a fight with you and he reckons he can do you," a bully would swerve it. He'd be thinking, "Sod that. I could get found out here and people will realise that I'm not as hard as I'm pretending to be," and he'd avoid the big handy cunt that was looking for him. Whereas if you said to Chris Little that some right handy cunt was looking for him it'd be like a red rag to a bull. And like a bull would, he'd go charging straight at them.

A good example of this was when he was sat in his house one night and his house phone rang (mobiles weren't as common then) and Chris picked it up and it was a lad that he knew and the lad said that he'd just been in a pub on Edgeley, the Windsor Castle I think it was, and that two blokes who looked a bit tasty and who he'd never seen before had come in and they were asking people, "Who's this fucking Chris Little?"

They would soon find out.

Now any bully who got a phone call saying that ONE tasty looking bloke was looking for him, let alone two, would give it a wide birth. Chris however jumped straight in his car, no phone calls to any of his mates for back up, and went straight to the pub. And within seconds of walking in the pair of them were out for the count. He'd sparked them both.

Now that clearly isn't bullying. Those two fancied their chances and they came unstuck and there were many more like them too, like the three at Shakers night club who turned up who Chris wouldn't let in.

All three of them had right attitudes, one in particular.

If you ever went to Shakers, which was on Didsbury road in Heaton Mersey (I think it's a kids nursery now) you'll remember that there was like an arch way that you walked through to get to the entrance and these three were stood under it pissing against the wall. Chris saw them doing it and shouted over to them not piss there and to go around the back, and the main cocky one shouted back to him, "Fuck off, we'll piss where we want."

I was surprised Chris waited for them to put their cocks away before hitting them! But wait he did.

When they'd finished pissing they came walking up to the door to get in and Chris told them to fuck off. I couldn't believe they had the gall to even try and get in after what they'd said. Any normal person wouldn't speak like that to a doorman and then expect to waltz in would they? But that gives you an idea of what these three were like.

One of them then said to Chris, "Tell you what. How about me and you go around the back on the car park and if I come walking back and you don't we go in. And if *you* come back we'll leave." And Chris said, "I've got a better idea. The same deal but *all three of you* come around the back. And if you're the one's that come walking back you can all go in for free AND I'll buy your beer all night." They agreed. And they all went around the back of the club onto the car park.

No prizes for guessing who came walking back! Chris had chinned all three of them and left them in a heap. Asleep!

Another one that happened at Shakers was when this bloke turned up who had a similar attitude to the three just mentioned. Chris wouldn't let him in either so this bloke said that he'd have a fight with Chris and told Chris that he'd let him have the first punch for free. I don't think Chris could quite believe what the bloke was saying. And nor could I! So Chris said to him, "Say that again?" And the bloke said, "I'll let you have the first punch - then I'll start fighting." And I looked at him and thought, "Hmmm, something tells me there won't be much fight left in you after Chris has had his free punch!"

So Chris said, "Okay," and stepped off the step. He then said to the bloke, "Are you ready?" and the bloke replied,

"Whenever you are." And so Chris took his free punch. And the bloke's head nearly came off!

As you may have guessed, the fight the bloke was anticipating didn't happen.

Chris worked on the doors of all the 'rough houses' and he was the first one landlord's called if their pub or club was getting a bit out of control. He was actually given his first job on the door by Dennis Cotterill. He'd only just turned twenty at the time, which is young for a doorman, but Dennis, who was the head doorman at a nightclub in Stockport at the time had heard of Chris's reputation and decided to give him a chance.

On Chris's first night, which was a Saturday, at around midnight a coach load of lads from the North East turned up. They'd been on a stag do nearby and they were staying in Stockport. There was around thirty of them and straight away as soon as Dennis saw them getting off the coach he told the other doorman that they weren't coming in. The last thing he wanted was thirty pissed up Geordie lads piling into the club that was already packed full of pissed up local lads! It would have been a recipe for disaster. So when they got to the door he told them that they weren't coming in. The lads weren't happy and an argument started. It was obvious how it was going to end; in a massive ruck.

As the Geordie lads were shouting at the doormen, threatening to smash the club up if they didn't let them in, Dennis saw Chris walking off towards the rear doors of the club, taking his black jacket and dickie bow off as he did so. Dennis thought to himself, "Fucking hell! He's bottled it!" and thought, "I knew it was a mistake taking a young kid on." And he was annoyed with himself because he thought he'd made a lack of judgement by giving Chris the job.

But he thought wrong. And it turned out that his judgement was spot on.

As Dennis and the other doormen were arguing and jostling with the Geordie lads they noticed that one or two of them in the middle started dropping to the floor. They then noticed two more drop to the floor. Then all of a sudden they heard a voice shout, "Fucking come on then!!" and a circle opened up in the middle of them all. And when they looked they saw Chris stood there with his shirt sleeves rolled up knocking them out! Dennis said they were dropping like skittles! It then dawned on Dennis that the reason why Chris had taken his jacket and tie off and sneaked out of the back of the club wasn't because he'd bottled it, it was so that he could work his way into the middle of the Geordie's in order to start knocking them all out! And he sparked about nine of them!

Ironically, after his murder, in one of the Sunday Newspapers Chris was compared to someone from the North East, the well known Middlesbrough hardman Lee Duffy.

Like Chris, Lee Duffy also had a fearsome reputation as a fighter who feared no-one. He was an ex-boxer like Chris was too and of similar stature. He was of a similar build as Chris as well weighing around 17st and over 6ft tall.

The photograph of them in the paper also showed them both in similar poses.

Lee was one of the most feared men in the northeast. And again, like Chris, he's still talked about now thirty years after his death. He's considered part of Teesside folklore and various books have been written about him. He's also talked about in other books such as Operation Sayers by Steve Wraith and The Tax Man by Brian Cockerill both of which are really good books. Documentaries and films have also been made about him, the most recent being Too Far Too Soon which was released in 2020.

Similar to Chris again, Lee made quite a few enemies and there were three attempts on his life before his death which happened in 1991 when he was stabbed during a fight. Apparently, the person who stabbed him, David Allison, was his friend. During the trial stories of Lee's violent past were revealed including how he used to play Russian Roulette with a loaded gun. Even Chris wasn't that brave! Or daft! David Allison was found not guilty of both murder and manslaughter as it was ruled that he'd acted in self-defence.

At Lee's funeral hundreds of people lined the streets in his home town to pay their respects to him and it was said that two lorries were needed to carry the floral tributes. That was the one difference between Lee and Chris. When Chris died they didn't line the streets to see him off and to pay their respects. In truth most were glad he'd gone. And those who were seen hovering near the church were only there to gloat.

One other funny one happened at the Fir Tree, the pub in Reddish where Chris was working on the door at the time, and although the bloke on the receiving end of it came across as though he was looking for trouble it transpired that he wasn't looking for it after all.

I was stood talking to Chris just inside the door and I saw this car pull up on the car park and a bloke get out of it. He was quite a big bloke and he didn't look like he was coming in for a pint. He wasn't *strolling* up to the door, it was like he was walking with a purpose. It's hard to describe what I mean, I just got the feeling he wasn't coming in for a drink and when he came up the steps he said, "Which one of you is Chris Little?" And as he said it he put his hand inside his jacket pocket. Quick as a flash, bang! Chris hit him and he dropped like a sack of spanners. He was out cold for about ten minutes and when Chris started to bring him around the bloke said to him, "What did you do that for?" So Chris said to him that he thought he was going to pull a gun or a knife out and the bloke said, "No. I wasn't. I've just come to give you that twenty quid that you lent my son last week and to say thanks and I was just getting my wallet out to give it you!" Chris had lent his son twenty quid the previous Friday so he could go to the Reddish Leisure Centre up the road for a drink and his dad had just come in to give it him back! Chris apologised and told him he could keep the twenty quid and bought him a pint.

He also had a fight one night at the Reddish Leisure Centre which ended in carnage. Two or three people also ended up in hospital, and I ended up there myself.

We'd gone in there after the Fir Tree and as I was stood at the bar waiting to be served I heard these group of three or four blokes having a discussion about who would win between a boxer and someone who did martial arts. They were mates and they weren't arguing, they were just having a friendly discussion and one was saying that he thought a boxer would win and another was saying that he thought a martial expert would win. As soon as I heard the conversation I knew that if Chris heard it someone would end up getting chinned but not for a minute did I imagine just how bad it would end.

As we'd come in I'd gone straight to the bar but Chris had stopped at the door and he was having a chat with the doormen. So having heard the conversation the blokes were having I thought I'd go back to him and make some excuse that it wasn't that busy or that there wasn't anyone in that we really knew and to go to Shakers instead. But as I started to walk over to him someone said, "Alright, Nick," and I turned around. I stopped and had a quick chat with them and when I turned back Chris was stood next to me. He'd also heard the conversation the blokes were having and he said to them, "What's that you're talking about?" and one of them said to him that they were discussing who would win between a good boxer and a good martial arts expert and Chris said, "Well it's obvious, the boxer would win," and one of them said, "Well not necessarily." I could see where this was going so I said to Chris, "It's shit in here tonight Chris, let's go to Shakers instead." And he said, "No. I'm interested to know why he thinks a martial arts expert could beat a boxer."

The conversation got more heated, the upshot being Chris said that he was a boxer and that he'd beat anyone who did martial arts and one of them replied that he did martial arts and he didn't think Chris could beat him. He was a game lad no doubt. So they went out into the foyer to sort it out.

To cut a long and violent story short other people got involved as well and Chris ended up battering - and I do mean battering - about four or five of them. Two or three of which, myself included, ended up in hospital with noses bitten off, eye sockets smashed in, cheek bones and jaws broken, gaping wounds that needed stitching and other injuries. And I ended up having twelve stitches in my bottom lip after this lad who was with these other lads who Chris was fighting with smacked me, and it was a belter. I had whiplash for a fortnight he hit me that fucking hard! I could've done with a neck brace never mind a dozen stitches. I dropped to my knees with blood pouring from my mouth and I thought, "I'm not fucking having that," so I got up and went after him. And he did it again! Even harder! So then I thought, "Fuck that. I'm not going back for thirds. I know when *I'm* beaten!"

But even though those stories are examples of him knocking people out and not being a bully, though he did go over the top in that last one - then again that was Chris when it came to fighting; there were no half measures - there were also those he knocked out that he didn't really have too. He even wanted to knock me out the first time he saw me!

It was in a squash club that used to be in Reddish which was also a nightclub at weekends and I went in there one

Saturday night. I was into bodybuilding at the time and with me being as big as I was and having a shaved head I must have looked a bit 'thuggish.' I'd never seen Chris before and as I was looking around the room I just happened to make eye contact with him and he glared at me - the type of glare I was talking about earlier. A mate of mine who was stood next to me said, "That's Chris Little," so I nodded at him - and he just blanked me. The twat!

A couple of weeks later I saw him in the Fir Tree where he was working on the door and I got chatting to him and we eventually ended up becoming best of mates.

At the time he was still a professional boxer and he was earning his money from working on the doors. He also did a bit of building work, as did I, and we set our own building company up.

Well, when I say we set our own building company up all we did was put an advert in the local paper and got a few flyers printed. We called it C & N Builders, the C standing for Chris, the N for Nick. We got some business cards done too and Chris thought it'd be a good idea to put the slogan 'the builders that care' on the cards, so we did, although what we should have put was 'the builders that couldn't care less.'

We were fucking useless!

Chris could just about put a concrete fence post in, and not a very straight one at that, and I'd only just finished a bricklaying course and some of the walls I built weren't very sturdy to say the least. Humpty Dumpty wouldn't have risked sitting on one of my walls! Talk about bodge it and scarper. Not that we scarpered. We just stood there pissing ourselves laughing - and still wanted paying!

We had two jobs on the go once, one was laying a few flags, the other was pointing the front of a house. So I went and laid the flags and Chris started the pointing and when I'd finished laying them I went back to the house where Chris was and when I looked at what he'd done I couldn't believe the mess he'd made of it. Cement was all over the brickwork and running down the wall!

When I got there Chris was stood in the front garden looking at it and when I got out of the car he said to me, "What do you think of that then?" And he said it as though I'd be impressed with what he'd done. He actually thought he'd done a good job. It was like he was stood there admiring it and that he was proud of his work.

I said to him, "Are you having a laugh?" and he said, "Why? What's wrong with it?" I said, "What's wrong with it? What's RIGHT with it! Look at the fucking state of it. The bloke wanted it pointing not rendering." And I said, "What did you use to put the cement inbetween the bricks with, a pointing trowel or a fucking catapult!"

We spent the rest of the afternoon cleaning it up and wiping it off the wall with rags and we just about got away with it.

Another job we did, or rather bodged, was when we were rebuilding this bloke's chimney stack. It was a Sunday morning and when we got all of the gear out of the car we realised that we didn't have any red dye to mix in with the mortar so it would match the rest of the brickwork on the house.

The problem was that in them days places like B and Q and Wickes didn't open on a Sunday like they do now and seeing as how we needed to finish the job so we could get paid we had to try and come up with a solution.

It was about 8 o'clock in the morning so I said to Chris lets go to the cafe over the road and get a bacon butty and a cup of tea and have a think about it. "Good idea," he said (any excuse for him to sit down and not do any work was a good idea!) And it *did* turn out to be a good idea.

So we went in the cafe and ordered two cups of tea and a couple of bacon butties. We then sat down at the table and pondered how we were going to get the red dye to finish the job. And as we were sat there racking our brains, not that either of us had much brains to rack, particularly when it came to building, the woman from behind the counter brought our bacon butties over. So I got mine and took the top slice of bread off it and then picked up the tomato sauce bottle that was in front of me to squirt some on it. But as I was about to squeeze the bottle Chris grabbed hold of it and snatched it out of my hand and said, "Use brown sauce, not that." I said, "Fuck off! I like ketchup on my bacon butties! Give it me back you cunt." And he said, "No, use the HP instead. We'll mix this in with the sand and cement. It'll make it go red!"

We did have some brains between us after all!

And that's what we did. We finished our bacon butties, nicked all the bottles of tomato sauce off the tables, went back and mixed it in with the cement, got our catapults out and finished the job!

The bloke we did the job for was none the wiser either. He actually gave us a twenty quid tip for doing such a good job. Happy days! Although he did have a slightly puzzled look on his face when he saw a dozen empty bottles of Tomato Ketchup in the skip!

They *were* the happy days too looking back. And at that time Chris was a totally different person to what he was towards the end. And believe it or not he was well liked then too. Yes, he was feared, but so too were other tough blokes around the town. And even though he was chinning people then and knocking them out left right and centre the difference was that he wasn't going out of his way to do it as he sometimes did in his latter years, and 99% of the time it was warranted such as when he was working on the doors or if someone fancied their chances. Or, as all hard men do who want to be known as the hardest man in their town, they make a point of chinning all the other hard men.

I'm not putting Chris in the same bracket, though I dare say he would've had a fight with them, but read Lenny Mclean's book or Roy Shaw's book, they did the same thing. They made it known that they were the hardest. And they did it by chinning anyone who had a reputation or who they viewed as a challenge. As did Jimmy Swords who I mentioned at the beginning, he said the same thing in *his* book. If he knew someone had a reputation for being a tough guy he'd go and chin 'em to let them know he was the main man. (By all accounts Roy Shaw turned down the chance to fight Jimmy Swords for fifty grand.)

But even though those 'building days' were happy days they were also a turning point in Chris's life - though to be honest he had no choice but to turn really because it was blatantly fucking obvious from the off that he wasn't cut out for a life in the building game! He'd have never have got his Master Builder certificate that's for certain! And I remember the day the turning point came.

It was shortly before the collapse of our building 'empire' which collapsed quicker than most of the things we built. We were digging a trench one day for a drain (that we didn't have a clue how to lay!) on a farm near High Lane in the village of Disley near the Peak District where Chris was living at the time and it was pissing down and freezing cold, and Chris said, "This is shit. What the fuck am I doing this for? I'm the hardest man in Stockport yet others are making all the money, and I'm stood in a fucking hole in the middle of a fucking field, knee deep in shit, piss wet through holding a fucking shovel." He then paused for a minute, like he was mulling things over in his mind, and said, "Fuck it. I'm gonna take the town over." And he did. And from that day on his reign - some would say of terror - began. Mind you his venture into the world of drug dealing and criminality didn't get off to the best of starts because the person he laid his first nine bar on fucked off with it! (A nine-bar is a block of weed that weighs 9oz. And 'laid on' means to give it to someone to sell.)

When Chris found out what had happened he was livid but I pissed myself laughing when he told me and I didn't half take the piss out of him. He was working on the door at the Fir Tree and he'd given it to a lad from Reddish called Kurt Flitcroft to sell. He was alright Kurt. He was well known around Reddish and he was a bit of a rum cunt too, rummer than most thought as it turned out! There weren't many who would have tried to have had Chris over, but have him over Kurt did and when Chris gave him the weed he disappeared with it and he never saw him again! What made it even funnier was that one of Chris's favourite films was Scarface with Al Pacino and he'd often watch it and I'd shout things across the room to him in the Fir Tree like, "Oi, Al Pacino, where did your weed go!" And he hated it and he'd shout back, "Fuck off Fisher you big eared cunt!"

I don't think he ever caught up with Kurt either. If I remember rightly I think Kurt ended up in Wales somewhere and I heard he died a few years later of a heart attack.

Looking back on it now that incident could well have been the catalyst for Chris turning the way he did as in him becoming more ruthless and brutal because I remember him saying to me (as I was laughing my bollocks off at him) that he'd make sure no-one ever dare do that to him again. And it wasn't long after that that he started becoming more violent and more intimidating. But in the end it proved to be his downfall.

In the Sticks And Stones Will Break Your Bones But Concrete Lintels Do A Far Better Job story the guy makes a very good point. And it's that if you intimidate someone and back them into a corner in order to achieve whatever your aim is, always leave them an 'out.' In other words, leave the person you've backed into a corner an opportunity to walk away perhaps thinking they've saved face or got off lightly but at the same time you get what you want. In the instance he talks of it was about a debt he was collecting for someone. Some fella owed fifty grand but he told the fella that the debt had gone up to seventy five grand. It hadn't, he just said it had. He also told the fella that he'd been instructed to give him a good hiding. Again, he hadn't, he just said that. The fella began panicking and he was wishing that he'd have just paid the £50k that he owed because now, in his mind, he was going to have to pay £75k AND he was going to get a pasting. So the guy lets him stew. He then says to him that if he pays the fifty grand within a week (which he's getting half of) he'll forget about the other twenty five and he won't give him a good hiding. The fella agrees, he's also mightily relieved. And he goes from being backed into a corner with seemingly no way out to walking away thinking he's done alright out of the deal, when in actual fact he hasn't. And the guy who backed him into the corner has got what he wanted without throwing a punch or using violence. It's a clever way of doing it. But that wasn't Chris's style. It was his way or no way. And his way was the violent way. The problem is, and this applies in general not just to what Chris sometimes did, is that if you keep on intimidating people and you keep backing them into a corner and don't let them out, sooner or later the person you're doing it to is going to think, "Fuck this. I've had enough" and decide to do something about it. And if someone isn't *physically* capable of doing anything about it they'll resort to other means.

Without doubt Chris changed once he got involved in the world he did and who knows, if he'd have stuck to just using violence towards people who were involved in that world, where after all it goes with the territory, then he may well still have been alive today, or at least lived a lot longer than he did. But in the end his list of enemies was bigger than his list of friends and I think he knew himself his card was marked. He obviously did know, hence his 'I want to live until I'm 31' comment in that interview. But as the saying goes, you live by the sword you die by the sword, and he knew that. He actually started carrying a sword with him, a big 3ft one which he had down his trouser leg one day and I couldn't quite believe my ears when he said he a 'good reason' lined up for carrying it if the police ever stopped him.

I came home one day and when I walked in Chris was sat there chatting to my mum. He'd just called around out of the blue with some chocolates for her, he'd also been over to my sister's and gave her a card and fifty quid to get something for her baby that she'd just had (there was a good side to him despite what some might have said) and after my mum went out of the room he said, "Here, look at this," and he stood up and pulled the sword out of his tracksuit bottoms and started waving it around like he was Zorro! I told him that if he got pulled by the Police he'd be fucked and he said, "Nah. It's okay. One of my neighbours who's an old lady said that she'll say I was on my way around to hers to cut her hedges for her!" He was being serious too! I nearly laughed as much as I did when Kurt fucked off with his weed! If he had a pair of garden shears tucked in his tracky bottoms he might have got away with it but not a bastard sabre!

Not long after that I went working in Germany bricklaying (my bricklaying skills had improved since our

C&N Builders days, but only slightly!) and I only saw Chris every couple of months when I came home for a week or two. So for the last two years of his life I didn't see him as often as I used to although I often rang him. I rang other mates too and more often than not they'd say, "Have you heard what Chris has done," or "You're not gonna believe what Chris has done now." And when I once rang him and asked him how things were he said, "Same old, same old. I've not been up to much." I then rang another mate and he asked me if I'd spoken with Chris recently and I told him that I'd just got off the phone to him and that he'd said he'd not been up to much. My mate sounded a bit shocked and said, "He's not been up to much? He's put two in hospital today, and one yesterday. He hit one of them with a claw hammer and he shot one of the others in the legs with a crossbow. He's also had half the town burnt down in a show of strength to the police and caused over a million pounds worth of damage. It's been all over the news!"

Just a normal (violent) day for him then! And that's how it became in the end - violence was 'the norm.'

As well as making a lot of enemies Chris was also upsetting some very 'capable' - and very dangerous - people including the Quality Street Gang. Barry McConnell was friends with a lot of the QSG and they asked him to get a message to Chris to 'reel things in.' So Barry got in touch with me and asked me would I pass the message onto Chris and I said I would though I said to him, "But you know what his answer will be don't you?" and he replied, "Yes, I've got a good idea what it'll be." And when I told Chris he said, "Tell them to fuck off. It's my town and I'll do whatever the fuck I want in it." Whether or not Barry relayed the message back to the Quality Street Gang I don't know though knowing Barry I don't think he would've done, which would have been the sensible thing to do because the consequences would have been dire. It'd have been World War Three - in Stockport!

As I've already said, after his death much was written and said about him and some of the things people said made me laugh. I don't mean made me laugh in a humorous way, it was a figure of speech, though some of the things said *were* laughable. They say never to speak ill of the dead. There are exceptions of course - Adolf Hitler and Jimmy Savile spring to mind! But on the whole why do it? So why some people came out with things like, "He knew not to bother me because he knew I'd have leathered him," or "I remember when my mate chinned him and put him on his arse" or "He started on me one night and I knocked him out," was beyond me.

Another mate of mine, Gary Slattery, who was also a mate of Chris's summed it up when he said to me, "Don't waste your time arguing and fighting with them. They're kidding nobody. The only people they're kidding are themselves."

But I wasn't the only one to have a pop back when people said those kinds of things, some of Chris's other mates did too. And as hard to believe as this may sound even one of those who was accused of Chris's murder stuck up for him on more than one occasion and put people in their place - both verbally and physically - when they started mouthing off and talking bollocks about Chris.

Old adversaries too let bygones be bygones. A couple of years after his death Gary Slattery was at a funeral at Stockport Cemetery where Chris is buried and after the funeral he was at he went and visited Chris's grave. And stood with him were some very well known Manchester 'gangsters' who in the past hadn't seen eye to eye with Chris. Nonetheless there they were paying their respects.

And the truths, the myths and the lies that were said and written about him? Well I've already said the truth, Chris did do a lot of things that he didn't have to do and he hurt a few that he needn't have hurt. As for the myths, well two spring to mind. I've already dispelled one actually and that was that he first started selling drugs when he was at school. He didn't. Though you could say he made a schoolboy error giving drugs to Kurt to sell! The other became a myth but started out as a lie. A lie created by the police. (The police, lie? Heaven's above. Surely not! And it's funny how when the police told of the night outside Hamilton's Nightclub they forgot to mention about how one of their CID officers used to regularly meet Chris behind the club and take envelopes of money off him.)

Anyway, the night in question (at Hamilton's) where the myth/lie originated from happened shortly after Chris had been released from prison for the attack on Liberty's Nightclub in Sale (It's too long to put here, Google it – it's another extremely violent one!) And he'd rang the police to say that he was having a bit of a 'get together' to celebrate his release - and about *three hundred* of us got together! It was just (another) show of strength really. He wanted everyone to know, including the Police, that he still ran the town.

I always remember - as does a mate of mine, John Stringer, who was stood next to me - when we were all outside the White Lion pub at the bottom of Underbank in Stockport town centre where we'd all met up and Chris was stood on a beer crate addressing everyone telling us where we were going etc. Hamilton's being the final port of call. And when he'd finished speaking I jokingly shouted to him, "Eh Chris, this is just a trick really. We're not here to back you up, we're all going to batter you." And he slowly looked around at us all - all three hundred of us - like he was doing some kind of head count, shook his head slightly, gave a wry smile and said, "Nah, there's not enough of you!" And he meant it. And if push would've come to shove he'd have jumped off that beer crate and weighed into the lot of us. And probably won!

But the myth / come lie - and this has appeared in numerous other books too - is that when we got to Hamilton's Chris approached the police who were all standing in a line right across the front of the club and said to the main one, the Superintendent or Chief Inspector, I'm not sure what rank he was, "Shake my hand and they'll be no trouble. If you don't the town will get wrecked." And it was said that the officer pointed at Chris and shoved his finger in his chest, as though he was laying the law down to him, and in a forceful manner said to him, "I'm not shaking *your* hand," and that whilst pointing at Chris, Chris grabbed his hand and shook it and then turned to his 'entourage' and punched the air in victory. And the officer later said that he was mortified that Chris had grabbed his hand and made it look like he'd willingly shaken it. But what he said, and what was reported, wasn't true. It happened nothing like that.

Part of what the police said had happened *was* true, the copper *did* refuse to shake Chris's hand but he certainly didn't point at him. Both of his hands remained on the brass handled wooden staff he was leaning on and he was far from forceful when he spoke, he spoke calmly. And when he refused to shake Chris's hand Chris told him that he'd regret it. The officer who was stood next to him, who also looked like he was of equal high rank then said to Chris, "*I'll* shake your hand Chris if you promise me they'll be no trouble," and Chris told him that there wouldn't be any trouble and the copper shook his hand. Chris *then* turned to all his mates and gave a punch.

I think that was the only time I saw Chris throw a punch without someone getting knocked out!

So despite what the police, the media, and other books said, the officer *willingly* shook Chris's hand. And how can I be so certain that's how it happened? Well because I was stood next to Chris and stood right in front of the coppers and I saw exactly how it happened and heard every single word. (And more than one copper later said how frightening it was and that they were shitting themselves at the thought of what might happen.)

Rumours did circulate that the police were behind Chris's murder. But they weren't. It was just silly gossip. Though I did hear one copper say that he'd have Chris shot.

It was in Stockport Magistrates court and we were sat in the cafeteria that they had in there waiting to be called to go up in front of the magistrates and there was a copper sat on the table opposite us reading a newspaper. Chris knew he could hear us talking so he made a throw-away comment and said, "I'll have that cunt shot." The copper didn't even look up from his newspaper, and knowing that we could hear him, he muttered, "Not before *we* have *you* shot."

Not long after, Chris *was* shot.

One of the lads that was with us in the magistrate's court that day, Steve, had a brother-in-law who was a copper. His brother-in-law was a member of the 'TAG', the Tactical Aid Group, or the TAU, Tactical Aid Unit as they're known now. They're the ones you see at football matches and at marches and protests that have the potential to turn violent. Most of the coppers in the TAU are built like brick shithouses and they don't fuck about when they arrest you! If they ask if you're going to come quietly you'd be advised to say yes! And when the rumours started going around about the police being involved in Chris's murder Steve told his brother-in-law what the copper had said about having Chris shot and his brother-in-law said, "No. We wouldn't have had him shot, definitely not. The way we would have done it would have been to have got him in the back of the van and knelt on his neck and suffocated him and say that he was resisting arrest."

Doesn't THAT sound familiar? (George Floyd)

And as for the lie that very nearly got The Stockport Express burnt down I'll leave that one for you to figure out for yourselves because even now it doesn't warrant a comment. But to give you a clue, in the part about Reddish I make reference to a certain nonce school teacher and a certain China man, and to brand someone the same as those types just because the reporter who wrote it had been threatened by Chris was quite disgusting. But yet again, that's the media for you. They don't care what they write and they don't care if the people's families they're writing about read what they've written - as long as it sells newspapers. The pen is mightier than the sword as they say. Even mightier than the sword Chris kept down his tracky bottoms that he used to cut hedges with!

But whether you liked him or loathed him, Chris Little will go down as a huge part of Stockport's history and they'll probably never be anyone quite like him ever again. And even though some said Stockport was a better place without him, at the outset he did have Stockport at his heart, and when he turned professional as a boxer he said in another interview he did, "I'm going to put Stockport on the map."

And he did. Although not quite in the way he originally intended.

When I was a kid I always used to look forward to Thursday's because it was the day my Nana used to come around after she'd been to Stockport. She'd go every Thursday without fail and she'd go in Marks and Spencer's and she'd buy cream cakes from the food hall for us. And more often than not when she'd come in the first thing she'd say was, "It was murder in Stockport today," referring to how busy it was.

It's vastly different now to what it was back then. It's nowhere near as busy. Even that eyesore 'The Red Rock' entertainment complex that they've built has made no difference. Who the fucking hell designed that! Whoever did wants shooting. I'm only saying that metaphorically by the way for anyone from Stockport who's reading who possesses a gun or who has access to them, of which there are quite a few of you, and who may take that comment seriously! Please don't shoot the designer of the building. (Burn it down instead!) And if the designer himself happens to be reading, what on earth gave you the idea to build such a monstrosity? Oh, and congratulations on winning the Carbuncle Cup for it. The Carbuncle Cup for anyone who isn't familiar with it is an architectural award - that no designer wants to win – and is given each year to the worst designed building in Britain and the Red Rock won it in 2018 where it was described as a 'garish, soulless shed!'

The 'precinct' as it used to be known in them days isn't exactly a ghost town now, although my Nan would be in for a bit of a shock if she ventured into Stockport on a Thursday - or any day for that matter nowadays - and saw how empty and quiet it is compared to back then. And if my nana was still alive today and called around to our house after going to Stockport, instead of her walking through the front door with a box of cream cakes (that she'd have to get from the Pound Bakery because Marks & Sparks, like most other shops, has shut down) and saying, "It was murder in Stockport today." She may well say, "I've just *seen* a murder in Stockport today!"

Stockport isn't the murder capital of the UK by a long chalk but it has had its fair share. There's been a couple of dozen at least since the 1970"s. There's been about half a dozen in Reddish alone where I live that I can think of.

Most of the murders have been well documented but there's been one murder in Stockport that not many will be familiar with, partly because it took place in 1861. Although the story did make it into the newspapers more recently in 1993. The reason being was because it was identical to the murder of James Bulger, the two year old boy from Liverpool who was abducted, tortured and murdered by two older boys that year.

It happened on Hillgate and two eight year old boys, Peter Barratt and James Bradley, killed two year old George Burgess, who, like the killers of James Bulger had never set eyes upon him before. And like the murder of James Bulger did, the murder of George Burgess also shocked the nation at that time. He'd been suffocated and his naked and badly beaten body was found lying face down in a ditch on Hillgate. Witnesses said that they'd seen the two boys throwing rocks at the little boy and hitting him with sticks, identical to the James Bulger case. The inquest into his murder took place at what was then called 'The White House Tavern' on Hempshaw Lane and the boy's body was kept in an outhouse at the back of the Tavern. So even back then murder wasn't uncommon in Stockport. And in the 1980's and 1990's when I used to go drinking around Stockport it wasn't uncommon to see people lying face down on Hillgate either – you'd usually see them around four o'clock on a Sunday afternoon on the pavement outside the Sun and Castle after they'd fallen out of there pissed!

As well as Stockport having the odd murder or two (dozen) and being home to the infamous and the slightly dubious, it's also home to the odd celebrity or two and the rich and the famous. And quite a few films and television shows have been filmed here as well. Who remembers the war film 'Yanks' staring Richard Gere and Vanessa Redgrave that was filmed around the market place and on Hillgate in the late 1970's? They saved a few quid on that film by shooting some of the gun battle scenes on Sunday's. And the reason they filmed those types of scenes on a Sunday was so that they didn't have to pay extras to play the parts of fallen soldiers lying face down dead - they just filmed the drunks who were lying face down unconscious outside the Sun and Castle instead who *looked like they were dead*!

Life on Mars was also filmed around Stockport as was Early Doors (filmed in The Grapes on Heaton Norris) which starred Craig Cash. And 'Sorted' starring Will Mellor, along with quite a few other television series, was also filmed in parts of Stockport, as is The Real Housewives of Cheshire. (Yes, I know the last one is Cheshire really but let's just say it's Stockport as it makes us look a bit posher!)

The sitcom Men Behaving Badly which starred Martin Clunes and Neil Morrissey was originally to be set in Stockport too, although in the end it never was. The producers of the show must have changed their minds after visiting here looking for suitable locations to film and saw that there was enough men behaving badly in the town as it is!

But The Real Housewives of Cheshire aren't REAL housewives are they? I'm sure they're all very nice ladies but they're not real housewives. I can't picture Dawn Ward in my mind, or any of the others for that matter, being on their hands and knees on the kitchen floor with their arses in the air scrubbing the lino can you? Though I dare say it'd be a very nice sight. Mind you, I often do picture Dawn Ward in my mind being on her hands and knees with her arse in the air - in a line with all the other Housewives of Cheshire - only they're not scrubbing the kitchen floor when I picture them in that position!

So not only can I not imagine the real housewives scrubbing the kitchen floor, I can't imagine them cleaning the oven either or going around the house with a cloth doing the dusting and then doing the hovering and then tidying everywhere up. Come to think of it *my* wife doesn't do any of that either. Which explains why our house is a complete shit tip!

She's a bit thick my wife you know. I was working on my car the other day and I asked her to stand behind it to check if the indicators were working properly and when I switched them on I shouted to her, "Are they working?" And she said, "Yes, no, yes, no, yes, no, yes!"

As well as celebrities and the rich and the famous, numerous premiership footballers live around here too. By 'around here' I don't mean Reddish or Brinny'! I've never seen many premiership footballers or multi millionaires or television stars hanging around Brinnington or Houldsworth Square. And when you read the part about Reddish it'll become even more obvious why they *don't* hang around Houldsworth Square!

I mean 'around here' as in the borough of Stockport, namely Alderley Edge and Wilmslow where most of them tend to live. Although I would imagine that most of the people that live there put their address down as Alderley Edge *Cheshire* not Alderley Edge *Stockport*! Though Alderley Edge and Wilmslow do have Stockport postcodes (SK9)

Alderley Edge and Wilmslow are lovely places to live, before we continue though, talking of footballers, here's another interesting fact for you. Did you know that once upon a time Stockport was home to the world's most expensive 17 year old footballer?

In 1985 Liverpool paid a quarter of a million pounds for Wayne Harrison when they signed him from Oldham. (Everton, Nottingham Forest and Manchester United were also interested in signing him.) Wayne also held the record at Oldham as being the youngest ever player to play for them at just 16. But after signing for Liverpool his career was blighted with injury and he was eventually forced to retire when he was twenty three after suffering a knee injury. He was another good lad. He was always smiling and laughing whenever I saw him. Wayne died seven or eight years ago and Liverpool legends Kenny Dalglish and Phil Thompson were at his funeral.

Not only are Alderley Edge and Wilmslow lovely places to live they are also two of the most *expensive* places to live, anywhere in England. And which is why I won't be moving there anytime soon. "Thank fuck for that," residents of Alderley Edge and Wilmslow cheer!

Those two areas are constantly in the top ten most affluent places to live in the UK and they're very much sort after places to live which is why it attracts the celebrities and what have you to live there. Some of the estate agents around there even have waiting lists for some of the really big houses. But as well as celebrities from outside the area coming here to live, over the years Stockport has produced its own celebrities and famous faces including sports personalities, singers and actors such as Will Mellor, Michelle Keegan, Ricky Hatton, Danny Miller, Craig Cash, Tess Daly, Yvette Fielding, Phil Foden, Sarah Harding, Lee Boardman and Mike Yarwood to mention but a few.

Angela Rayner, the Deputy Prime Minister also comes from Stockport. Proper Stockport lass! She makes Johnny Vegas sound posh!! She'd be right at home in 'Benidorm' too! Though by all accounts she prefers Ibiza. And judging by that video she'll need to brush up on her dancing if she's got aspirations of appearing on 'Strictly'!

Stockport is also the 'adopted' home of comedian Jason Manford who's originally from Salford. Someone else from Salford who also looked upon Stockport as his home was Paul Medati who used to run Masters, the snooker club and nightclub. Paul was a professional snooker player. I used to play with him regular. I rarely beat him, even with a 21 point start off him, and I wasn't a bad player myself years ago. I once had a century break too, 107, so I was an okay player, but he was too good for me. Paul was a top bloke, he really was, and I don't know anyone who had a bad word to say about him. We had some belting nights in Masters. Sunday nights were always good. More often than not we'd stay in there after it'd had closed and we'd fall out of there at about five in the morning. Wrecked!

Everyone who knew Paul, or went in Masters will have stories to tell either about him or something that happened in there and one particular story made the headlines many years ago. It was when Alex 'Hurricane' Higgins turned up at a tournament with a black eye and the excuse he gave to the press for getting it was that a horse had kicked him. When really, Paul had given it him. Alex Higgins used to practice in Masters and the night before the tournament he was in there and a row started between him and Paul. Paul had said something about Higgins's his ex-wife, Lynn, which Higgins took offence too. Words were exchanged and they started fighting which resulted in him getting a black eye off Paul. It also resulted in Paul's wig coming off. In his book Higgins said that he thought he'd scalped him when it came off! They soon made up though. I remember another time when Alex Higgins was in there and he was playing in the match room with Paul and Jimmy White. The match room used to back onto the end of the bar and there used to be an opening like a window, or a serving hatch if you like, where you could order your drinks and they'd pass them through to you. You could see this opening from the main bar and me and my mate, Wayne Halliday, were sat at the bar having a drink. At the time it was reported in the papers that Higgins was taking cocaine, and he appeared at the serving hatch and asked for a coke, and Wayne quietly whispered to me, "I wonder how much he wants, a gramme?" I started laughing, and like a knob I repeated it, and I shouted over to Higgins, "How much do you want Alex, a gramme?" And he went mental! He came storming out of the match room and flew up the corridor to where me and Wayne were sat and screamed, "I don't fucking take drugs! Look. Look up my fucking nose," and he lifted his chin up and stuck his face right in mine so I could see right up his nose. He then stepped back, put one finger on his right nostril and said, "If I took coke I wouldn't be able to do this would I," and proceeded to blow his nose. And a hurricane of snot came flying out of his left nostril and landed all over the bar. And all over me! I could've done with having a face mask on that we've all been wearing for the last few weeks as it would've caught half the snot that flew in my face!

That's my claim to fame – I've been snotted on by Alex Higgins!

I said to him, "Calm down you cunt, it was just a joke," and he shouted, "I don't fucking like jokes like that," and stormed back in the match room. However even though Higgins didn't appreciate the joke, Paul did, and when I looked through the serving hatch I saw him stood there pissing himself laughing. Jimmy White had a smirk on his face too.

Another time Paul pissed himself laughing at something I did was one Saturday morning when I'd gone in there for a game of snooker. I think his son Steve was there too. And 'Slim', one of the doormen, was also there. Me and Slim we were always winding each other up and playing daft tricks on each other, and like I did, and still do, Slim liked to have a bet on the horses. Part of this is an old joke but Slim still fell for it. I said to Slim, "Eh, Slim. I've got a horse for you today. It came in last week at 10/1 and it's out again today at Ascot." He said, "Is it? What's it called?" So I gave him the name of this horse, only it had no chance of winning. One of the donkey's on Blackpool Beach, and a lame one at that, would have had more chance of winning!

All I'd done was look at the paper that morning and picked the worst horse that was running that day. I told him that it was a reliable tip and that it'd romp home and said to him, "Trust me, it's worth sticking a few quid on it." And the idiot *did* trust me and he went straight to the bookies and put fifty quid on it!

He came back about twenty minutes later with a big smile on his face and showed me and Paul his betting slip and said, "I stuck fifty on it. If it comes in at 10/1 that's five hundred smackers I'll have." And laughing, he said to Paul, "And if it *does* come in you can fuck off an all because I won't be working tonight!" and wondered off across the room. And as he walked off Paul said to him, "Oh you'll be working tonight alright. You'll have to to get that fifty quid back that you've just thrown away," and started laughing. And Slim *stopped* laughing!

Slim looked at me and disappeared, then a few minutes later he came back with a newspaper. He was looking at the racing pages and he said to me, "You lying cunt. You said that fucking horse came in at ten to one last week. I've just looked at its form and it's never won. It's lost its last ten races." So I said to him, "I'm *not* lying. It *did* come in at ten to one. The only problem was that all the other horses in the race came in at half past twelve!" And he said, "You fucking big eared cunt Fisher!" and stormed out. Paul was wetting himself laughing and as Slim was going out of the door Paul shouted to him, "And don't be late tonight either!"

And no, the horse didn't win!

I did another good one on Slim when he was working at Yates's on the Market. I hadn't seen him for a while and me and my mate Rob Owen went in there one Saturday night. He was pleased to see us and he said, "Alright Nick, how you doing? How are you Rob? Good to see you," and he took a twenty pound note out of his pocket and gave it us and said, "Here, get yourselves drink."

The fool must have forgotten about the wind ups we played on each other!

Back then lager was about £2 a pint so he'd have been expecting £16 change, but instead he got a penny!

We were just going to get two pints but when the barmaid came over I said to her, "Have you got any champagne?" and she said they had and that it was £19.99. So I looked at Rob and said, "Shall we?" and he started laughing and said, "Yes!" So I told her we'd have a bottle and I asked her to put it in an ice bucket and fill it with ice just to rub it in on Slim a bit more, and she did. And I asked her for two champagne glasses as well. Rob then asked her for a tea towel and we told her what we were doing and she laughed and gave us one. I gave her the twenty quid and she gave me a penny change. Rob then draped the tea towel over his forearm and picked up the ice bucket with the champagne in and we walked back over to Slim with it. He was looking the other way so Rob went and stood against the wall and I tapped Slim on his shoulder and when he turned around I said to him, "Thanks mate. Here's your change," and gave him the penny. He looked at it in the palm of his hand and said, "What the fuck's that? Where's the rest of it?" And I laughed and nodded towards Rob. And Slim looked at Rob stood against the wall looking like a wine waiter from the Savoy Hotel, holding the ice bucket with the champagne in it in one hand and two champagne glasses in the other, with the tea towel draped over his forearm, and he shook his head and said, "I don't fucking believe it. I've fell for it again!"

Slim did get one over on me though shortly after that at Masters, and Paul Medati was in on it. It was a warm night and we were stood near the entrance talking. They had a security camera in the car park and it was at the top of a steel pole that was about 15ft high. Slim said to Paul, "How long did it take you the other night to shimmy up that pole, Paul?" And Paul said, "I can't remember. Was it twenty seconds?" Slim said, "I think it was, I'm not sure," and then said, "But I know *I* did it in twelve seconds." I said, "Bollocks. You've never climbed to the top of that in twelve seconds." And he said, "I have - I bet *you* can't do it in twelve seconds." So I said, "A tenner says I can," and he said, "You're on."

So I went and stood on the wall next to it and Slim said, "When I say go, go. And I'll time you," and he said,

"Ready? Go!" And I jumped on the pole, grabbed hold of it with both hands, wrapped my legs around it and started to climb up it. And I got about six foot up it and slid straight back down it again - it was covered in anti climb paint! And it was black!

I was covered in it. It was all down my shirt, which just happened to be white, all down my trousers, all over my shoes, on my hands, on my face - it was all over me. Slim was howling laughing and Paul had to get his hanky out and wipe away the tears he was laughing that much. What goes around comes around as they say! All good fun though.

Paul died in 2008 and there were loads at his funeral. One or two professional snooker players were there too including John Virgo who said a few words at the service. Also present was Graham Jones who used to play snooker in Masters with Paul and myself. Graham is also dead now and it was only fairly recently that he died. And in a roundabout way I suppose it's because of people like Graham - and the thousands of others that have died over the last few weeks - that I wrote this book. And that's because Graham, like the others, was a victim of the coronavirus. And if it wasn't for Covid I probably wouldn't have written it. Like everyone else, I've been stuck at home with not a lot to do so I thought I'd write a book.

Graham wasn't that old either, early fifties maybe, and he was fit and healthy and he kept himself in good shape too. In fact it was only last year that he entered a senior's bodybuilding competition. And so it just goes to show that if the coronavirus can take people like him out - and take people out half his age who are probably a lot fitter - it can take *anyone* out. And that's why you should take no chances – I'll be masked up and gloved up whenever I go out, or whenever I go shopping at least, until this shit's gone that's for sure.

Just to side track for a moment (again.) The Covid really has brought the best out in some people, fund raising, helping neighbours and so on. But it's also brought the worst out in some people too. There really are some right selfish cunts around and some of the behaviour I've seen in Morrison's in Reddish is disgraceful. It's not that bad now but when everyone was panic buying (which to a degree I can understand because at the end of the day you've got to look after you and yours) some of the abuse the Morrison's staff were getting was unbelievable. They were doing the best they could and they could only put on the shelves what they had in the back. And having a go at them just because there was no fucking baked beans, like one prick was doing one day, is uncalled for. It wasn't *their* fault there was hardly anything to put on the shelves, and as soon as they put out what they had, it went! I went in there one night and not only were there no beans left there was literally fuck all else left either. We had a tin of minestrone soup and a packet of Wotsits between the four of us for our tea that night! I soon got pissed off going in there in the evening and there being nothing left so I thought I'd go during the day instead, and so the following day I did and when I got there it was absolutely hammered. I thought they were filming Supermarket Sweep in there when I went in! Every cunt was charging up and down the aisles just grabbing what they could. They probably didn't need - or want - half of what they were getting, they were just getting it for the sake of it. And what was that all about with the bog roll? Why was everyone stocking up on *that*? People were filling their trolleys with it. Why? The coronavirus doesn't give you the shits does it? We all shit ourselves at the thought of getting it but it doesn't literally *make* you shit! Even if it did give you the shits there are plenty of other things you could wipe your arse on apart from bog roll if you get stuck, like newspapers, magazines, the endless take away menus that get shoved through your letter box, and this book! (Which one of you cheeky fucker's just said my books *aren't fit* to wipe your arse on!" My books have been read by royalty and at Number 10 Downing Street I'll have you know.)

Hopefully we'll soon be nearing the end of this shit (I'm on about the coronavirus, not this book, there's still another forty pages of this shit to go!) and a bit of normality will start to return. Although when it does I think some people won't be quite as welcome in their local supermarkets as they once were. And as one of the women on the check out in Morrison's in Reddish said to me as I was paying for my shopping: "I've seen people in a completely different light and some of their behaviour is shameful. The way some people shop and the amount of food they buy is just selfish. It's pure and utter greed. Some people think only of themselves and don't give a damn about others. As long as *they're* alright they couldn't care less if there's nothing left on the shelves for anyone else. They really wouldn't care less if others starved." And I said to her, "I totally agree with you love. Some people are way, WAY too excessive with the amount off shopping that they're buying."

She then said, "That'll be one thousand two hundred and fifty seven pounds please!" And I paid, pushed my nine trolley's full of shopping back to my car, loaded it all into the trailer that I'd attached to the back of it and fucked off home with it all!!

As everyone from Reddish knows, the Dragon Palace, the Chinese restaurant on Gorton road, used to be called Chings. I forget the name of the couple that owned it, presumably Mr and Mrs Ching! And the lady used to be a keen photographer and she used to take photos of places around Reddish such as Houldsworth Square and St Elisabeth's Church and Reddish Vale Country Park. And she'd have them imprinted onto the table mats that the plates were put on when your meal was served. And below each photograph were the words 'No Place Like Reddish.' These words were quite apt as there probably *isn't* a place quite like Reddish anywhere else in Stockport. For a start Reddish has some of the most well known landmarks in the borough such as the Country Park and Houldsworth Mill which was once home to the mail order giant John Myers. Over the road is another well known landmark, Broadstone Mill, which when completed in 1907 was the largest cotton spinning mill in the world (the previous biggest was Houldsworth Mill which was completed a few years earlier.) And it's said that Reddish Working Men's Club on Greg Street is the oldest working men's club in the country, the steward of which 'Tats', Mark Taylor, makes everyone feel extremely welcome when they go in there - everyone that is apart from me and my mate Rob. And unlike others who go in there and are met with a friendly smile and a "hello" by Tats when they enter, whenever me and Rob used to go in there we were greeted with, "Who the fuck let you two in?!" This was partly down to our previous escapades and (extremely) high jinks which made the pair of us extremely unwelcome in most pubs. It also made Mark -

and most other landlords - extremely nervous whenever we entered their pub!

Something else you probably never knew about Reddish is that it was once listed as one of the best places in the UK to go 'cottaging.'

Cottaging, for those of you who are unfamiliar with the term, is gay slang for anonymous sex between men in public toilets. Uncannily, how I found out what cottaging was, was when I was in a public toilet myself. I was at Victoria Coach station in London. It was in the early eighties and I'd gone down to London to meet a bloke called Pete Brennan from Reddish who was working down there. Pete was a plasterer and he said he'd give me some work labouring for him so I went down to see him. I went by coach, one which had no toilet, and when I got off it I was bursting for a crap so I went in the toilets for one. I put my rucksack down in front of me and sat down, and as I was sat there I noticed a magazine on the floor. It wasn't a glossy type magazine like 'Hello' or 'OK', it was more of a independently/ home printed A5 size booklet type thing.

It was open, and on the page there was a photograph of the outside of some public toilets and I recognised them straight away. They were the ones opposite Morrison's in Reddish. They're still there now. Well the building is at least, but the toilets are no longer open. Take a look next time you're coming out of Morrison's after you've done your shopping. Right opposite is the bus shelter and behind it you'll see a small single story building, and that's them.

So I picked the magazine up to look at the photograph and under the photo was an article saying why it was a great 'cottage' and it described the various activities that went on in there. One was where someone would go in and sit down on the toilet and put a bag or a briefcase in front of them. Another bloke would then come in and stand with his feet in the bag and the one sat down would suck him off. The reason they'd stand with their feet in the bag was so that if anyone looked under the bottom of the door where there's usually a gap they wouldn't see the person's feet and it'd just look like someone was sat down having a crap with their bag in front them. Although if anyone 'in the know' looked under the door and saw a bag or a briefcase on the floor it was a sign that the person in there was 'up for a suck!'

And as soon as I read that I picked my rucksack up sharpish before someone looked under the door, got the wrong idea and came in and shoved their cock down my throat!

Another thing they used to do was stick their knobs through a hole that they'd made in the partition and some bloke in the cubicle on the other side would give them a nosh or toss 'em off. Or back onto it even! It was obviously the thrill of doing it in public that was the attraction and it probably still goes on today, though personally I can think of better places to be sucked off than in some disgusting public toilet whilst standing in a pool of someone else's piss! But each to their own.

However it wasn't only gay men that did it/(do it.) Straight men did it too, some of whom were married.

The work with Pete never came off and I ended up coming back home and working on a building site in Manchester and on the site were some lads from Liverpool and they were the rummest cunts I've ever met, even rummer than Kurt who disappeared with Chris's weed! They were into everything, knocked off gear, fraud, scamming, you name it they were into it, but they were good lads. And I was telling them about the toilets in Reddish and one of them, Carl, said, "We'll have to go there one day for a laugh," and one of his mates said, "Just go over the road instead," and pointed at some toilets that were there and said that he'd seen quite a few blokes going in and out of there during the day and that he thought it was a bit odd why it was so busy. So we watched it for a few days and we saw that the same blokes seemed to be going in and out of it.

In the article in the magazine where it said that a sign that someone was a willing participant for a blow job was a briefcase or bag between their feet, it also said that another sign was that if when you looked under the door you saw that someone was stood side on with their feet facing the partition between the two cubicles, that was also a sign indicating that they'd give you a suck and all you had to do was stick your knob through the hole that had been purposely made in the partition. And, if you went in the cubicle they were stood facing and a penis was sticking through the partition then that was indicating you were free to suck it, pull it, or stick your arse on it. But what it certainly wasn't indicating was that you could grab it with a pair of pliers and twist it!

Before we go any further I just want to say that I'm not, and never have been, and Carl wasn't either, homophobic, because no doubt some knob, no pun intended (well it was actually) reading this will think "fancy doing that, it's well out of order doing that to someone just because they're gay." Well we *didn't* do it because they were gay, it was just a bit of a laugh that's all, though I doubt very much the bloke who it happened too saw the funny side! I also had no idea Carl was going to do it either.

Like I said, the same faces used to go in and out of there, one of whom was a bloke who looked like he was in his early fifties. He was always smartly dressed. He looked like the businessman type, suit etc, complete with briefcase (surprise surprise!) He came at around the same time most days, three o'clock'ish, so one day at around quarter to three me and Carl went in there. I stood on the toilet seat and Carl stood facing the partition in front of the hole that had been made in it. The reason I stood on the seat was so that when the bloke looked under the door he'd only see Carl's feet facing the partition and it'd look like he was up for a 'bit of fun.' And sure enough ten minutes or so later someone came in. We heard him shuffling about outside the cubicle we were in where presumably he was looking under the door. We then heard him go into the cubicle next door and we heard the sound of the zip on his trousers going down. Then all of a sudden a penis popped through the hole!

We were dying not to laugh and I honestly had no idea what Carl was going to do. I didn't know what we were going to do to be honest. I thought maybe shout "pervert" and start laughing and run off, or slap his cock, or flick it. Or gob on it! And then run off. I really didn't know - but

Carl did. And as I'm stood on the bog seat with my hand over my mouth trying not to laugh Carl pulls a pair of pliers out of his back pocket and slaps them on the bloke's cock and starts squeezing it! The bloke screamed, as you would if some fucker clamped a pair of snips on your bell end and squeezed them as hard as he could! And as he squeezed the bloke's cock, Carl shouted, "Give us your fucking wallet!" I looked at Carl and held my arms out as if to say, "What the fuck are you doing?!" And he just shook his head and whispered, "It'll be alright," and laughed. All I could hear from the other side was the bloke shouting, "Agghh, Agghh" in agony, and then he said, "Okay, okay" and he kicked his wallet under the gap at the bottom of the partition. I jumped off the bog, unlocked the door and ran out, followed by Carl who'd grabbed the bloke's wallet and ran behind me laughing his bollocks off, and we darted back on the building site and hid.

I couldn't believe he'd done it. The poor bloke had only gone in there to get a quick blow job and ended up nearly having his cock torn off! That was the first and last time I did it but Carl and his mates did it loads of times. They actually went to the lengths of finding out where other 'cottages' were and did the same thing. They even got bank cards off some of the blokes and demanded the pin number, and while one of them, usually Carl, clasped the fella's cock with the pliers the other would dash to the cash dispenser and withdraw two or three hundred quid out or whatever they could get.

I suppose it was the perfect crime if there is such a thing as those fella's who were on the receiving end of it couldn't really go to the police and report it or go home and tell their wives what had happened could they. Could you imagine walking into a police station if it happened to you saying that you wanted to report a crime and when the desk sergeant asks what happened you said, "Well I was in these public toilets and I stuck my cock through a hole in the cubicle so another bloke could suck me off..." You'd probably get arrested yourself! Also, if you were married, which no doubt some of those blokes would have been, you couldn't have told your wife what had happened either. So if you're a married woman reading this and you've always wondered why your husband withdrew a few hundred quid out of your joint bank account one day many years ago and he was reluctant to explain what he'd done with it, and when he got in bed that night you noticed he had plier marks on his knob, now you know why!

What made me chuckle was that in that magazine they said that the toilets were located in 'the village of Reddish in Cheshire.' And anyone reading it who's never heard of Reddish would probably conjure up images in their mind of Reddish being a traditional English country type village like you'd expect a village to be in somewhere like Kent or the Cotswolds with thatched roofed cottages and quaint tea rooms centred around a picturesque village green that had a duck pond in the middle of it and a cricket pitch adjacent to it, and where nothing disturbs the peace apart from the trickle of a stream and a blackbird singing merrily as the sun goes down. And those who did conjure up images in their mind of Reddish being like that would've been in for a bit of a fucking shock when they got here! Because Reddish is fuck all like that!

For the benefit of anyone who has never been to Reddish it isn't quite your traditional English country village. For a start it isn't centred around a picturesque village green with a duck pond and a cricket pitch. Our 'village green' is Houldsworth Square, and it's not so much green but more of a dreary grey. There are no duck ponds or cricket pitch's either, although it has been known for people to be attacked with *cricket bats* in our village! And there are no quaint tea rooms. Instead we've got two charity shops, four pizza, kebab and burger takeaways, half a dozen nail bars, two shut down banks - soon to be three - and a needle exchange. And the closest you'll get to any thatched roofed cottages is the Thatched Tavern pub. Though we do have a few benches dotted around our 'village green' for people to sit on and relax and take in the wonderful views, not that there are many wonderful views. The only slight problem with the benches is that you'll never get to sit on one because invariably they're taken up from ten o'clock in the morning onwards by the local piss heads who sit there swigging cans of cheap shitty lager that they've just bought from the village off licence. West Coast Wines! And as for the sounds of trickling streams and blackbirds merrily singing, these are replaced by the sounds of wailing police sirens as they race to McColl's supermarket that's situated opposite the village green after it's been held up at knife point. For the third time in a fortnight! So describing Reddish as a village is pushing it a bit to say the least!

But I wouldn't go as far as comparing Reddish to Rhyl like one journalist did a few years ago. It was the other way around actually and he said that Rhyl was like "Reddish by the sea!"

Rhyl was alright when I was I kid. It's gone downhill now but at the time it was great. Everyone went there. Most of the people I know who are my age used to go there for their holidays. We used to go every year. We used to go on the train because my dad didn't drive because he had epilepsy. He liked a drink too so it's just as well he didn't drive because epilepsy, alcohol and cars aren't a particularly good mix. So rather than get in a car with an epileptic piss head behind the wheel we stuck to the train.

My dad was the type where everything had to be on his terms. And everything was done in his own time and when it suited him. He was a fucking selfish pig headed cunt basically! And one year as we boarded the train he decided to get off to get a newspaper and I remember my mum saying to him, "No, Barry, don't. It's leaving in a minute." And he turned around, and in his slow, deliberate tone that he spoke with he said to my mum, "It'll *wait* for me."

I was only six years old at the time but even *I* knew it wouldn't wait for him and I looked at him thinking "I bet it fucking doesn't you silly cunt!"

But the daft bastard got off anyway and went to get a paper and as he was casually strolling back to the train with his Daily Express under his arm the train began to pull away. And he stopped and looked at it like he was in disbelief that the driver had the audacity to leave without him. And as I looked out of the window I could see him berating someone from British Rail on the platform because the train had gone without him.

He was unbelievable. He actually thought the train would wait for him, like the driver would be sat there thinking "Fuck the timetable. And fuck everybody else on the train. We can't leave because Barry has to get his Daily Express!"

My dad finally turned up in Rhyl three hours later after catching the next train. Although he may as well have stayed where he was because after we'd unpacked and were strolling down the sea front we saw a coach with 'Mystery Tour' on it. So we asked my dad if we could get on it and he said yes and two and a half hours later we were at Belle Vue in Gorton which was about two miles away from where we lived!

My dad had nodded off on the coach and woke up just as we arrived and when he saw where we were I heard him mutter, "I don't fucking believe it."

Belle Vue by the way for those who aren't old enough to remember it or haven't heard of it was just like Blackpool pleasure beach. It had roller coasters, rides, water slides, fun fairs and a zoo. It also had a concert hall where a lot of the big names and bands played, Rod Stewart being one of them.

Even though I've been to Rhyl loads of times, my wife never had. She's from down south and she'd heard me talk about Rhyl a few times so I said I'd take her. And we went one day. And she never wants to go back ever again! When we used to go there for our holidays we used to stay in a B&B on John Street. So when we got there we had a stroll up to it to see what it was like now. And after what we saw I don't blame my wife for not wanting to go back!

Rhyl has got one of the biggest drug problems in the UK and apparently the area around John Street is / was well known for dealing. Ella, my eldest daughter, was two at the time and we had a stroll down the sea front and got her an ice lolly and watched Punch and Judy for a bit and then carried on and turned into John Street. She was in her pushchair and she had an ice lolly, and as we turned into John Street I heard this shouting and swearing coming from one of the houses just a little bit in front of us. I heard this voice shout, "I want my fucking gear you cunt, where is it," and then this other voice shouted back, "Fuck off, now, or I'll do you." And just as we got level with the house this lad came staggering backwards covered in blood and he fell onto a car bonnet. Then some other bloke appeared and started knocking fuck out of him with a baseball bat!

My wife was frightened to death and just wanted to go home straight away, though Ella just sat there in her pram sucking on her ice lolly looking at them knocking seven bells out of each other thinking she was just watching a slightly more violent version of Punch and Judy!

That was one of the last times we went to Rhyl. The earliest I can remember going was when I was about four years old and we went with one of my dad's friends, Ken Gooddy and his family. Steve was there, Ken's eldest son, and I remember my dad slipping and falling in the lake (he was probably pissed!) at Pontin's where we were staying, and I remember me and Steve pissing ourselves laughing.

I've been on holiday with Steve since and he said something one night when we were there that not only made me piss myself as much as I did when we were in Rhyl, I was laughing that much that I had to get up and walk out of the restaurant we were in. It was also the first time I've ever had Gaelic Prawns.

Have you ever heard of Gaelic Prawns? I hadn't either. Neither had I heard of Swat and Sore Pock (Sweet and Sour Pork) or Pecking Stalled Craspy Checkin (Peking Style Crispy Chicken) until we went in this Chinese restaurant in Santa Ponsa in Majorca.

There were loads of us there and at the end of this particular night, me, Steve and Swifty (Mark Swift) went for a Chinese. It was late on, gone midnight, and we were the only ones in the restaurant. I think it was about to close when we turned up but they let us in anyway. It was only a small place, a family run type thing, and the woman came over and gave us a menu each and we ordered some beers and then we looked at the menu. And as we started reading it we saw that it was full of spelling mistakes. Nearly everything was spelt wrong. Most of the dishes had a letter missing or the wrong letter had been used in the words so instead of it saying Beef curry it said *Bef* curry and instead of Garlic prawns it said *Gaelic* prawns and instead of it saying Fried rice it said *Fred* rice. And it had things like spring rules, and Satan checkin, which presumably was Satay chicken, and fred moshrooms in ooster sauce and barbiecued spared rips. Inadvertently, they'd even named a dish after Eric Cantona and instead of it saying Cantonese Style Roast Duck it said Cantona Stalled Rost Dock!

It looked like a kid had written it. And it turned out that one had.

We set off laughing at all the mistakes and you know what it's like when you're pissed you laugh even more at the silliest things. What made it worse, or better looking back, was that Swifty has got a really raucous laugh. He's got one of those infectious laughs that makes others laugh even more and the woman, who was stood watching from the counter and who probably wasn't overjoyed in the first place that three drunks had come in just as she was about to close, came over.

She must have realised what we were laughing at, and in an abrupt tone, and not in the best of English, shouted, "Why you laugh at my menu?" One of us, I forget who, apologised and gave some excuse that we weren't laughing at the menu and that we were laughing at something else. But she knew we *were* laughing at it. I bet we weren't the first ones to laugh at it either. No doubt every fucker that went in there pissed themselves when they read it!

So we tried our best to contain ourselves and not to laugh, but again, you know what it's like when you're pissed and you've got the giggles; once you start it's hard to stop. She was starting to get the hump and in an even more abrupt tone and in a loud voice she said, "You want order or not?" So inbetween bouts of laughter we said yes.

She really was getting annoyed now and she more or less shouted, "WHAT YOU WANT?" So trying not to laugh Steve and Swifty ordered theirs. She then looked at me and barked, "WHAT 'BOUT YOU?" And so with putting emphasis on the spelling errors I said, "I'll have the GAELIC Prawns and two spring RULES to start, and I'll have SATAN'S CHECKIN in OOSTER sauce and can you ask FRED if I can have some of his rice." And then I said,

"Oh, and do the BARBIE-cued spare ribs come with a doll?"

That was the final straw for her! And in her broken English come Chinese accent she screamed, "It's no funny! It's no funny! Don't make fun. My Son write menu. He only ten year old. He half Chinese half Spanish and cannot read or write plopply."

And Steve picked the menu up, held it in his hand, looked at me and Swifty and said, "That's handy 'innit. A Chinese menu written in English by a ten year old mixed race dyslexic Spaniard - no fucking wonder it's full of mistakes!" He then closed the menu, put it on the table, and said to the woman, "Just do me egg and chips. It'll be easier."

Well I started howling laughing. And I couldn't stop! I had tears streaming down my face and I nearly fell off my chair I was laughing that much! In the end I had to get up and walk out because I was laughing that much! And as I was walking towards the door the woman shouted, "Come back. You ordered food. Where you go?" So I said, "I've changed my mind. I'm going for a DOOOONER KEBAPPA instead!"

And here's another quick one from that holiday.

Swifty is a right thick cunt. That's a bit unfair actually calling him thick. He's actually got a very responsible job. He's the one that signs a plane off and gives it a safety certificate saying it's okay to fly, which is a bit worrying having seen some of the stupid things he's done! So he's obviously not thick, he just lacks a bit of common sense! He's a bit care free, in a world of his own. He's a bit like the aeroplanes he works on - his head's up in the clouds!

We were all in this bar watching the football on one of those big screens. United were playing in the Champions League and I was sat near him on a stool. He was slightly behind me and all of a sudden he shouts, "Yes! What a goal that was," and I looked around at him, as did everyone else. And the reason we all looked around was because on the screen *we* were watching the match on, no goal had been scored. The ball wasn't even in play because one of the players was down injured.

So I said to Swifty, "What are you on about? No-one's scored." And he said, "They have, there. Look. It was a belting goal," and he pointed to a different screen that he'd been watching the match on, only it wasn't the same match. And not only wasn't it the same match it wasn't even a real football match.

You know what it was? It was one of those big PlayStation gaming screens that you sit in front of and put a Euro in and play FIFA world football video games on!

The tit thought he was watching the United game and he was the only person in the bar looking at it. And as I was looking at it it showed a replay of the goal that he thought United had just scored. The 'player' ran from inside his own half, dribbled past all of the opposing team, and when he got to the edge of the box he flicked it up with his right foot onto his head, nodded it into the air and then turned around and scissor kicked it into the top corner of the net!

It would've been goal of the century let alone goal of the season if it was real! Lionel Messi, Ronaldo and Maradona couldn't have come up with a goal like that between them! And Swifty signs the docket saying that a plane is safe to fly! So if the next time you go on holiday you board the plane and see that it has been certified to fly by Mark Swift you might want to get off it and wait for the next one.

When I was in that Chinese restaurant I caught a fleeting glance of someone who I presume was the woman's husband and he was the spitting image of someone who you used to see around Reddish and other parts of Stockport when we were kids, a bloke nicknamed China Man Joe. Or *'China* Joe' as we called him. He was deaf and dumb and it was rumoured that he was a nonce and that he molested young boys. Whether there was any truth in it I don't know, it may just have been urban myth. It was also said that he used to carry a massive knife and that he threatened kids with it, though I never saw him get it out in front of me. I never saw him get his cock out in front of me either so it may well be all a load of bollocks about him being nonce! Then again, he might have *contemplated* getting his cock out in front of me but thought better of it because he was worried I'd grab it with a pair of pliers! However I did see something one night that makes me think there might have been some truth in what they said about him.

It was in what was then Reddish Boys Club opposite Reddish Vale School at the top of Vale Road near the Country Park. I was only about eleven at the time and me and a few of my mates were in there one night, and so was China Joe. Which, looking back now, was a bit odd.

There used to be an indoor five-a-side pitch in there that you could look down on from above and as I was watching two of the teams play I looked around towards the entrance of the club and saw two coppers come in. China Joe saw them too and he went and stood in a broom cupboard and left the door half open so he could see them. He saw me looking at him and he put his index finger to his mouth as if to say, "Sshhh, don't say anything."

The coppers spoke to one of the bloke's who ran the club and then left and when they did China Joe came out and the bloke went over to him. I thought nothing of it and turned away and carried on watching the five-a side and then China Joe came over to me, mumbled something, smiled, patted me on the head, stroked my face and gave me some sweets from out of his pocket and walked off. So maybe the rumours *were* true, who knows?

Now I know exactly what one person is thinking right now having just read that and that's Marv'', a mate of ours. And I know exactly what'll be going through his mind. Marv likes to 'elaborate' on stories slightly. He'd make a really good newspaper reporter actually because he never lets the truth get in the way of a good story. Particularly when the end result is that it ends up with someone having the piss taken out of them! And within days of this book being released I can guarantee that stories will begin to circulate that not only did I get patted on the head by China Joe, I got bummed off him too! Just like stories began to circulate that I got bummed off a certain school teacher when I was at school shortly after Marv had heard a story about something that had happened. Ironically the school was opposite Reddish Boys Club - Reddish Vale Comprehensive.

I put that story in another book that I wrote, although everyone knew about it well before then, including Marv. And Marv being Marv, he added a *bit extra* to the story, like he does, and spread it around that I was buggered by this teacher during detention! And he used to bring it up every Sunday afternoon in the Fir Tree pub in Reddish where we drank and everyone took the piss out of me! But whereas there is some doubt as to whether China Joe actually was a nonce who liked young boys, there is no doubt whatsofuckingever that this teacher was a nonce who liked young boys. Well, teenage boys at least. And if any ex-pupils or teacher's from that school beg to differ and say he *wasn't* a nonce then amongst other things why would he ask me how many times a day I masturbated and could I get an erection after I'd ejaculated and start masturbating again straight away? There was no touching or anything like that, the dirty bastard just asked a few questions. (Questions that had nothing to do with the subject of English Literature that he taught.) 'Mr Comb-over' as he was nicknamed - because of his Bobby Charlton style comb-over hair cut - also once came in the changing rooms and popped his head around the showers and told the boys of the under 13's football team that he 'volunteered' to manage to make sure that they pulled their foreskins back and wash behind them. He even 'jokingly' offered to wash our foreskins for us - like any responsible kid's football coach might do. Well like Barry Bennell might do anyway! Though no doubt Marv will tell you that this peado teacher *did* wash my foreskin for me. With his mouth!

The answers to Mr Comb-over's questions by the way are three times a day, and yes, I used to be able to maintain an erection after ejaculating and continue masturbating but not anymore! And take it from me, Marv's story about me and China Joe at Reddish Boys Club will be far better than the one I've just told you!

I was going to name the teacher by the way but my solicitor advised me not too. He also said it'd be best not to give any clues as to what his surname is either. So I won't. Then again, you probably won't NEEDHAM!

I mentioned the Thatched Tavern pub earlier, and many years ago the landlord of the Thatch was a bloke called Syd. He was a Manchester City fan and one Friday night my mate, Rob Owen, was in there and the following day City were playing Man United at Maine Road. Syd didn't know Rob that well at the time (or what fucking idiots me and Rob were!) and because he couldn't go to the match he let Rob have his two season tickets. The problem was that Rob was a United fan and Syd's tickets were for the City end but Rob promised him he'd be on his best behaviour (that'd be a first!) and so the following day Rob turned up at my house and said that he'd got two tickets for the match and did I want to go. His actual words were, "I've got some good news and some bad news," so I said, "What's the good news?" and he said, "I've got two tickets for the match." So I said, "And what's the bad news?" and he said, "I'm skint!" In other words, I was paying. All day!

So off we went. And at eleven o'clock we were in the pub and we ended up well pissed. Full of Vodka, the lot! In the meantime Syd was working in the Thatch and Barry McConnell and Steve Gooddy and Terry Gooddy and a few others had gone in there for a few pints before they too went to the match. Syd, who was one of Barry's best mates, told them he wasn't going because he had to work and one of them asked him what he'd done with his tickets and Syd said that he'd given them to a lad called Rob, and Barry said, "Rob? Rob Who?"

Syd said that he couldn't remember his second name but that he seemed alright and one of them asked Syd what Rob looked like and when Syd described him Terry said, "He wasn't called Rob Owen was he?" And Syd said, "That's it, Rob Owen." And they all looked at each other and chuckled. Barry then said, "And who did he say he was going with?" And Syd said that Rob had told him the name of his mate he was going with but that he couldn't remember it, so Barry said to Syd, "His mate wasn't called Nick by any chance was it?" And Syd said, "That's it. Rob and Nick." And Barry, Steve, Terry and everyone else who was stood at the bar started pissing themselves laughing and Barry said, "You've give your season tickets to Rob and Nick?!" And Syd said, "Yes. Rob seemed alright." And Barry said, "He is alright, and so is Nick - when they're not together. But when *they are* they're a pair of fucking nutcases! Then Terry said, "So you can kiss goodbye to your season tickets because they'll be getting confiscated by City!"

And Terry wasn't wrong!

We were sat near the front in the Platt Lane Stand, which was the City end, and behind us right at the back were a load of our mates from the Fir Tree who, like the rest of them in that end, were all City fans. Rob was dead easy to wind up, and United scored but he didn't celebrate, obviously, because we were surrounded by City fans. So I said to Rob, "You call yourself a proper United fan? If you were you'd get up and cheer and celebrate when they scored." And Rob thought about it for a moment and said,

"*I'll* get up and cheer if *you* get up." So I said, "Okay." Although I had no intention of cheering or celebrating when United scored - I just wanted to get Rob thrown out. For a laugh! Well that's what mates do, eh!

In the second half United were attacking the Platt Lane end where we were sat and Ryan Giggs came tearing down the wing, dribbled past a couple of City players and smashed the ball into the back of the net. So me and Rob both jumped up. But I sat back down again straight away and Rob didn't realise I had, and he started jumping up and down and shouting, "United! United!" and turned to where our mates from the Fir Tree were behind us and started shouting, "Fuck off you blue bastards. Fuck off!" whilst sticking his fingers up at them and laughing at them. Our mates just laughed at Rob, they thought his antics were funny, even though they weren't happy that United had scored. But the rest of the City fans were going mad, as you can imagine, and a few of them came running down towards us. Rob then turns around to me thinking I'm stood up celebrating with him, and he's laughing and jumping up and down. He then saw that I wasn't stood up and that I was sat down and I looked up at him and said, "Tatty Bye!" and waggled my fingers at him as if I was waving 'Bye Bye' - meaning he was going to get lobbed out! And I started laughing at him. He realised what I'd done and his face changed from one of joy to one of horror.

It's hard to describe the look he had on his face but if you can remember the Tom and Jerry cartoons when Tom was chasing Jerry and he runs around the corner straight into that big snarling Bulldog and Tom's face becomes stricken with fear, well that was the kind of look Rob had on his face!

The police came running in and grabbed hold of him and started dragging him out and as they were dragging him away, in a headlock, Rob shouted to them, "Throw that big eared cunt out as well, he's with me." (I wish I had a pound for every time I've been called a big eared cunt. I'd be a millionaire!) And this copper came hurtling up to me and shouted, "Are you with him?" so I said, "No mate. I'm not. He's a fucking nuisance, get him out. He's been like it all through the game." And the copper looked at me for a moment, a bit unsure, then said, "Okay," and walked off. And as he walked away I stood up and started chanting, "OUT, OUT, OUT, OUT," whilst pointing at Rob who was getting dragged out by two coppers. And then all the Platt Lane, about ten thousand of them, joined in shouting, "OUT OUT, OUT, OUT!!" And you could just about hear Rob shouting back, "You fucking big eared bastard!"

A couple of years later Andy Siddall, one of our mates brought a copy of GQ magazine in the Fir Tree and in it was a feature on football hooliganism. And whose picture was right in the middle of the page in full blown colour showing them being arrested at a football match and being thrown out? Rob's! At that game! It showed him being marched out of the ground with one arm up his back and underneath the picture they'd put a caption "I ain't done nuffink officer!"

*Not all of the following extracts are by the original author. Some are by people who contributed stories that were published in his books.

I've no idea who it was that came up with the phrase 'crime doesn't pay' but whoever it was certainly wasn't a criminal because as all criminals know crime *does* pay and it can pay very handsomely. A better saying would be 'crime is all about trial and error' because if you make an error whilst committing crime chances are you'll end up on trial for it and if found guilty you'll be punished by the courts. But some people who commit crime or who are heavily involved in it not only make errors, they make errors of judgement. And sometimes the consequences of making an error of judgement can be far worse than the consequences of just making an error, and in some cases it's not the courts who punish them for it. It's people like me.

'Enforcer' 'Hired Muscle' 'Henchman', there are various terms for people like myself. And unlike in the courts, in the world I operate in there are no guidelines or rules as regards to the type of punishment handed out. It's whatever the person who is paying sees fit, and the following will give you an idea of the kinds of things that can happen if you're involved in criminality and you cross the wrong people.

This particular one didn't directly involve me, I just happened to be there discussing another 'job' and I saw the end result.

I was with somebody in their office one day and as we were speaking his secretary came in and said that someone was here to see him. So he said excuse me and got up and left the room. I could see him speaking to this person through the door and when they'd finished talking he came back in. He sat down behind his desk and opened one of the draws and he took out a small jewellery type gift box and pushed it across his desk to me and said, "Take a look at that." So I opened it. And inside was a silver necklace and it had a pendant on it and dangling from the pendant was a finger. It was the little finger, and it had been cut off someone's hand, and the hand belonged to the fella who he'd just been talking too. And as I looked at it he said, "I don't know what to do with that. Keep it to show people so they'll know what lengths I'll go to, or give it back to him as a reminder not to fuck with me ever again."

The finger wasn't in its entirety by the way, as in with the nail and skin still on it. It was just the bone. It'd been completely stripped of all the skin and tissue and then it had been cleansed and mounted on the pendant. Where and who it'd been taken too to have it done I have no idea though I doubt very much he'd have got it done at Beaverbrooks or Pandora.

I suspect that it might have been quite painful for that fella having his finger cut off but it probably wasn't half as painful as what happened to the person whom I was there to discuss. I'm not going to divulge the reasons why this occurred, let's just say that in the eyes of the person who asked for this to be carried out they thought the person on the receiving end of it warranted such punishment. And his punishment was to have his legs broken.

The person who was to have his legs broken had actually been given an option, not by me I might add. And his options were either to have his legs broken or be kneecapped by being shot in both knees, and he chose to have his legs broken. So we broke them. We took him to a lock up garage - without a struggle, he went willingly - and we sat him on a chair. He put both feet up on another chair opposite and we asked him if he was ready. He said he was, so two of us picked up a concrete lintel that we'd had put there and dropped it onto his shins halfway between his knees and his ankles. The pain must have been immense. He screamed the place down, and afterwards, as instructed by the person who'd asked me to carry the job out, I arranged for him to be taken to hospital. A few days later the person who'd asked for it to be done went to visit him in hospital. I don't know if he took him a bunch of grapes and a bottle of Lucozade but he visited him all the same. He asked him how he was doing and the guy said that it wasn't as bad as it could have been as his legs weren't actually broken and that they were just partially fractured, which was surprising considering the amount of pain he was in. And so my 'employer' said to him, "They're not broken? Well in that case I'm going to have to do them again then aren't I." The guy thought he was joking, but he wasn't. And my employer reminded him of the deal which was that he was either kneecapped or he had both of his legs broken, and seeing as how his legs weren't broken the deal wasn't complete, therefore he'd have to have them done again.

Ruthless, maybe. But a deal's a deal. And so after spending the next ten weeks in traction, when he came out of hospital we broke them again. And this time they *did* break. In half.

We used the same lintel that we'd used before and we dropped it in the exact same place on his shins as we did the first time. We did more than drop it actually. We *slammed* it down, just to make sure. And because they'd already been partially fractured his legs just snapped. They were literally dangling by the skin and you could see the bone sticking out.

Job done.

Sometimes though just the *threat of violence* is enough to achieve results and there's no need to cut fingers off or snap people's legs in half. I also sometimes give people an 'out', an opportunity for them to settle up, or whatever, whilst at the same time leading them to believe that they've done okay out of it and that they've got off lightly. Here's an example.

I was once asked to get £50,000 back off someone, of which I was getting half. Taking half may seem a lot, and it's an old cliché, but fifty percent of something is better than a hundred percent of nothing. It was a business deal, a legit one supposedly, and this geezer had taken this other guy's money. But instead of investing it as he should have done he just fucked off with it. So the guy who's money it was asked me to get it back. It then became apparent that it wasn't the first time this person had taken money off people and not done what he should have with it. And because things were getting a bit hot for him he upped sticks and went to Canada and when he was there he opened a steak house with the money he'd conned out of people. But his *mis*take was thinking he couldn't be found. But the world's a small place these days and you can be on the other side of the world in Australia or New Zealand in less than 24 hours. And you can be in Canada in less than eight. So me and a friend of mine paid him a visit.

We booked a table in his restaurant and as luck would have it, it was him that came over and served us and when he asked us what we'd like I said, "We'll have the 8oz sirloin with chips and two bottles of Bud please." He said okay and said that someone would bring the drinks over and that the steaks would be about twenty minutes, so I said that'd be fine. And as he turned to walk away I said, "Oh, and Michael, I'd also like that seventy five grand you owe Anthony."

He looked like he'd seen a ghost.

He completely shit himself and the first thing he said was, "I don't owe him seventy five grand, I only owe him fifty." Straight away I had him. He'd admitted he owed it. So now was the time to put pressure on him.

I told him that the other £25,000 was interest that Anthony had added to it. He hadn't added it to it, I just said that. I also told him that I'd been instructed by Anthony to give him a good hiding. Again, I hadn't, I'd made that up too. Now he *really was* panicking because going through his mind he was thinking that not only did he have to pay the fifty thousand back that he'd took, he was also going to have to pay a further £25k on top. PLUS he was going to get a right pasting.

I could tell by looking at his face that he was about to fill his pants. He was getting in a right state, which was how I wanted him to be. So I said to him, "I'll tell you what. If you agree to pay the £50,000 you owe I'll ring Anthony and ask him will he accept it and forget about the other £25,000. Also, if you pay it - and you don't fuck me about - I won't give you a good hiding."

He agreed. And he paid it within a week.

So sometimes, instead of using violence, using mind games that leads people to believe that they've done alright out of the deal is a better option and everybody's happy. Here, Anthony was happy because he got half of his money back. I was happy because I got paid £25k, and Michael was happy because he thought he'd got away with not having to pay an extra twenty five thousand and he'd avoided getting a good hiding.

And here's a tip for you to finish off with.

Be very careful what you say and who you say it in front of because it doesn't matter where you are you never know who might be listening.

I was at Barcelona airport once returning home from something I was doing in Spain for somebody and I was sat with my back to this guy who was on his phone. I wasn't ear wigging but I couldn't help but here what he was saying. He was discussing a business deal, part of which was to do with a large property development in South Africa and I heard a certain person's name mentioned. I knew of this person and he was at the top of the tree in our world and from what this guy was saying he was quite obviously dropping his name to whoever it was he was speaking to in order to sway the deal more in his favour. Dropping names, when you haven't been given permission to do so by the person whose name you're dropping, can land you in hot water. It's not something you do and you're either very brave or very fucking stupid if you do it.

So I got up and walked about ten yards in front of him and stood as though I was using my phone and as he was busy talking I took a photo of him and when I got back home I went to see the person whose name he'd dropped. I told him where I'd seen this guy and what I'd heard him say and said that I thought it may be of interest to him and showed him the photo I'd took. He said that he knew this person but that he had no connection to the deal or to the development. He asked me to send the picture to him on his phone, which I did, and I left it with him. He then did a bit of digging and he found out that the guy at Barcelona airport had used his name in order to get the better part of a multi-million pound deal from which he stood to make half a million. But he didn't contact him or say anything to him. Instead, he left it for over three years until the project was finished and everyone had been paid out. He then rang the guy up and asked him how he was doing and said that he hadn't spoken to him in a while and asked how things were. He said that he hoped all was well and made small talk with him. He then mentioned that he'd heard about the project in South Africa and that it was all finished and the guy said that was right and that he'd done very nicely out of it. So he said to him, "Yes, I believe so. And I believe you owe me £250,000."

The guy asked why would he owe him £250k when he had nothing to do with the deal and he hadn't put any money into it. So he explained about me over hearing him dropping his name at Barcelona airport three years previously and sent him the picture I took. He then told him that he'd spoken to other parties involved in the deal and they said that the reason he'd got such a big chunk was because he'd told them he had his backing, when in fact, he hadn't. He then pointed out to him that if it wasn't for him using his name he wouldn't have got such a big chunk - if any involvement at all in the deal - therefore he was entitled to half.

The guy then had no alternative but to pay up because he knew what would have happened if he didn't. This was one person you definitely *wouldn't* want on your case and having a finger cut off or a leg broken would be like having a slap on the wrist in comparison to what might have happened to the fella had he chosen not to pay. I also got a nice drink out of it too, which was very kind of him.

And so despite what the sticks and stones nursery rhyme might say about names never hurting you, some names *can* hurt you. Even if they only hurt you in the pocket. And sticks and stones may well break your bones but in my experience concrete lintels do a far better job.

As _ _ _ _ _ _ said in the story you've just read (I haven't named him as he asked me not too. I also didn't fancy having my legs snapped in half or have my fingers chopped off, so I didn't!) name dropping isn't the done thing and it's frowned upon by the 'main players.' who operate in the world he does – the underworld. Like he also said, if you're stupid enough to do it it can land you in a lot of trouble. It can also result in you getting a crack, as a devious cowboy builder found out when he tried ripping off my Nan'.

It was quite funny how it came about and it wasn't long after I'd come out of prison. I was round at my mums one day and my Nan called (with a load of Marks and Spencer's cakes!) She was talking to my mum in the kitchen and I heard her say to my mum that she was on her way to the bank to get the money out to pay the men that had repaired her roof. I didn't take much notice of what she was saying at first but then I heard my mum say, "I'll ring the police," and my nana said, "No, I'll just pay them." I then heard my mum say, "Well don't tell Nick."

My mum was obviously concerned that I'd do something, and she was right.

So I waited until my nana had left - so as not to worry my mum seeing as how I'd only just been released from prison - and I shot after her and caught up with her and asked her what was going on. And she said that earlier that morning some blokes had knocked on at her house and said that her chimney pots were loose and that they were about to fall off and said that for £150 they'd fix them for her, and my nana had said okay. But there was nothing wrong with the chimney pots. These blokes were just going around ripping old people off. And they didn't fix anything. All they did was take the chimney pots off my nana's roof and took them with them to sell! They were the big crown chimney pots that you see in garden centres that sell for about £100 apiece. So all they did was pinch her chimney pots and charged her £150 for doing so!

My nana said that they were coming for the money at two o'clock so I told her I'd be there.

I got to her house at ten to two and I told her to wait in the back room and just after two o'clock a transit van pulled up across the road and three blokes got out of it. They must have been a bit tired because one of them looked like he'd just woken up and he yawned as he got out of the van and another had a quick stretch. But I suppose they were entitled to be tired really weren't they? After all, it must be extremely hard work going around ripping off old age pensioners.

So after the one who had yawned had woken up (and who very shortly was going to be put back to sleep again) he walked over and knocked on the door and you should have seen his face when I opened it! He was expecting a frail, grey haired, little old lady to answer the door but instead a 6ft tall skinhead built like a brick shithouse with shoulders as wide as a barn door and arms like Popeye opened it! He must have felt like he was Little Red Riding Hood when he saw me and he must have been thinking, "My, what big muscles you have Grandma!"

He looked up and down the house and then looked at the number on the front door, and with a puzzled look on his face said, "Er, sorry mate, I must have knocked on the wrong house." So I said, "No, you've knocked on the right house but unfortunately for you the wrong person has answered the door," and I stepped forward and smacked him and sparked him right out. And before he'd even hit the deck, his mates, who saw what had happened, jumped in the van and fucked off and left him! I dragged him inside and when he came round I pinned him against the wall by his throat and I explained the situation to him, which basically was that he'd ripped the wrong pensioner off and that he wasn't getting paid. And that instead of my nana giving him £150, he was going to give her £150 for nicking her chimney pots. Whether he was still a bit dazed and confused and hadn't quite got over the shock of being flattened by muscle-bound Grandma I'm not too sure, but he started waffling on about how they'd done a "good job at a fair price" and wanted paying for it and he said that he wasn't going to hand over the £150. And then, rather stupidly, 'Little Red Riding Hood' said, "I'll get Chris Little onto you!" So I said, "Will you really?" I then proceeded to tell him how I was very good friends with Chris and that like most other people Chris despised those who went around ripping old people off. And, more worryingly for him, Chris, who really was a *big bad wolf*, didn't appreciate people using his name for their own benefit. And he gulped, put his hand in his pocket, took £150 out and gave it me! He also gave me an extra fifty quid and pleaded with me not to tell Chris that he'd dropped his name, which I didn't.

I first went to Brinnington in the mid 1990's and I swore then that I'd never go back. And I haven't! At the time I was a sales rep for a brewery and several of our pubs were located in the Greater Manchester area one of which was in Brinnington in Stockport. Manchester wasn't usually an area that I covered but due to staff shortages I had to go there and when I was chatting to one of the other reps and told him that I was going to Brinnington he started laughing and said, "Good luck!"

I knew someone who lived not far from Stockport and I'd planned to meet him later that day for a game of golf and he too made a wisecrack when I told him I was going to Brinnington and said to me, "Can you not swap your route with someone else!"

I later wished I had.

As a brewery rep you often visit rough pubs and more often than not the roughest ones tend to be on council estates which a lot of places like Brinnington are made up of. But even though the pubs are rough - and parts of the area where they're located are - on the whole the people who live there are nice people. Though the ones that frequented the pub I had to visit weren't very nice at all.

I should've had an idea as to what kind of place Brinnington was as I was driving on the main road into it because as I was doing so two lads on motor bikes came hurtling towards me on the wrong side of the road pulling wheelies with no crash helmets on and wearing balaclavas! And when I drove further into it I saw a horse come running down the road. On its own! And three other horses that looked like ponies were standing on the grass verge beside the road happily grazing!

I'd seen nothing like it in my life before. However I hadn't seen it all.

As I pulled up outside the pub and got out of my car a man walking his dog strolled past and he said to me, "Make sure you lock it if you're going in there." So I smiled at him and said, "Don't worry, I will!" And I *did* lock it. And although I locked it, which in hindsight was pointless, rather foolishly I'd left my golf bag and golf clubs on the back seat. They were expensive clubs too, just under £800's worth.

When I entered the pub I saw a group of around a dozen males aged in their late teens to early twenties sat in the corner of the room across from the bar and as I was chatting to the manager I noticed two of them get up and leave. And around ten minutes later they came back in again.

After speaking with the manager and doing what I had to do, I left. And when I walked out of the pub I noticed that the rear door of my car was wide open and when I got to my car I saw that my golf clubs had gone. Someone had forced the door open and pinched them. So I went back in the pub and told the manager and as I was talking to him one of the lads in the group that was sat in the corner shouted over, "What's happened mate?" So I went over to them and told them what had happened and the lad said, "If you want them back they'll be a finder's fee." So I said, "A finder's fee?" And he said, "Yeah, fifty quid - and you'll get your clubs back."

I couldn't believe what I was hearing! It was obvious what the two lads who had got up and left the pub had done; they'd gone outside, looked in my car, seen my golf clubs and nicked them. And they were charging me £50 to get them back! And when I asked the manager was there anything he could do he said, "Not really, no." So I had no choice but to pay because like the manager said it'd have been the last I'd have seen of my golf clubs if I didn't.

So having agreed to buy back my own golf clubs the lad I spoke to said that he'd "go and try and find them for me" and left the pub. And miraculously, no more than two minutes later, he came walking back in with them!

It's my own fault really I suppose for leaving my golf clubs on view on the back seat of my car for someone to see and pinch. But having to buy them back off the person who pinched them is a bit much!

If you've read the book I did called Gym'll Fix It you'll be familiar with the 'dildo' story that was in it and for some reason it ended up staying in the glove box in my car. And around twelve months later it was still in there the night I went to see Mike Tyson fight Julius Francis at the M.E.N Arena in Manchester in January 2000. What a waste of money that was. It was all over after a minute of round two. And when I got home I said to my wife, "That was a big disappointment, it was all over in a couple of minutes," and she said, "Now you know how I feel when we have sex!"

My wife is always taking the piss out of me about my performances between the sheets. She once installed a mirror on the ceiling over our bed so I said to her, "I didn't know you liked to watch yourself writhe and moan in ecstasy during sex?" And she said, "I don't, I like to watch myself *laugh* during sex." Even the postman knows about our sex life. He said to me the other week, "Your wife thinks sex is much better on holiday doesn't she?" So I said to him, "When did she tell you that?" And he said, "She *didn't* tell me. I've just read the postcard she's sent you from Spain!" And I once said to my wife, "I'd walk to the ends of the earth for you" and she said, "Yes, but would you stay there?" I think the reason my wife is like that towards me is because I upset her with something I said to her a while back. She was getting dressed one morning and she said to me, "Do these jeans make my bum look like the side of a house?" So I said, "No. The side of our house isn't blue!" And as she was stood looking at herself in front of the full length mirror in the bedroom she huffed and sighed and said to me, "I feel really horrible. I look fat, old and ugly. It'd be really nice if you paid me a compliment now and then." So I looked her up and down and said, "Your eyesight's fucking perfect!" She then said to me, "I'm going to spend £10,000 on implants to make my breasts bigger." So I said, "Why don't you save yourself ten grand and just rub toilet paper between your tits?" And she said, "Well that won't work will it." So I said, "Why wouldn't it? It works wonders on your arse." But like a lot of marriages do our marriage went through a bit of a rocky patch so me and my wife went to see a marriage guidance councillor, and in an attempt to find some common ground between us the councillor said, "Name one thing that you've both got in common." So I said, "Well neither of us sucks cock." And she once questioned if I was faithful to her. She said to me, "Tell me honestly, am I the only woman you sleep with? So I said, "Yes, *you are* the only one I sleep with – I'm up all night with the others shagging." She thinks she's clever too. I walked in the bedroom with a sheep under my arm one night and said, "This is the pig I have sex with when you've got a headache." And she looked at me and sarcastically said, "I think you'll find that that's a sheep." So I said to her, "I think you'll find I was *talking* to the sheep." Some of you might think I'm being a bit cruel towards my wife but I'm not the only bloke to take the piss out of her. She was in a nightclub once and this fella said to her, "You're the best looking bird in here." My wife was really made up with his compliment and gave a girly giggle and said, "Ooh! What makes you say that then?" And the bloke staggered sideways, hiccupped and said, "Eight pints of Lager, Six Rum and Cokes, Seven Sambuca's, Eight Tequilas and a bag of LSD!" But even though I regret getting married I do enjoy watching our wedding video, and whenever I watch it I watch it backwards because I love it at the end when my wife takes off her wedding ring, walks back down the aisle, gets in the car and fucks off! Though some blokes are devastated when their wives leave them and they get really upset. It happened to a mate of mine and he said to me, "My wife left me the other day. I've tried crying but tears just won't come out. What can I do to make myself cry?" So I said, "Imagine she's come back again." Equally though, a lot of blokes would love it if their wives left them. A pal of mine's numbers once came up on the lottery and he ran in the house and shouted upstairs to his wife, "Pack a couple of suitcases I've just won the lottery!" His wife shouted down, "Shall I pack for warm weather or cold?" And he shouted back, "I couldn't give a fuck what you pack just get out." And I read about one bloke who had a right stroke of luck in getting rid of his wife. He was out walking with her one day when they came across a wishing well so he leaned over it and threw a penny in it and made a wish. His wife then leaned over it and threw a penny in it and made a wish but she leaned over the well too far and fell in it and drowned and her husband said, "Fuck me, it works!" But despite the bickering and the swipes we have at each other my wife does give me cause for concern at times and she gave me a bit of a fright the week before last. It was a Sunday morning and she was in the kitchen cooking my breakfast and all of a sudden I heard a loud thud, so I ran in the kitchen and I found her lying unconscious on the floor. She'd collapsed and she wasn't breathing and she'd gone blue in the face. I panicked at first and didn't know what to do and I started to get really worried. Then I remembered - Wetherspoons do an all day breakfast for just £3.99.

As I said in Gym'll Fix It, my wife doesn't read my books. And it's just as well!

I went to that Mike Tyson fight with a couple of mates of mine, Tony Kendo and Mick Walsh (Mick was the son of Joe Walsh, the legendary hardman who the Quality Street Gang would call upon if they had any trouble.) We went in my car and on the way there I turned off the main road and started heading towards Reddish Vale Country Park which is situated in the middle of some woodlands. And as we were driving down this dark country lane Tony asked where we were going. So I told him that we were going somewhere quiet because I wanted to show him something, and said that it had to be somewhere out of the way so nobody could see what it was, and winked at him. And with a 'I know what you mean' look he replied, "Okay."

He was sat in the front and Mick was sat in the back and I drove down the country lane and pulled onto the car park. It was about 7.00pm and with it being January it was dark, so I put the interior light on. I then had a quick look out of the windows, making out I was checking that nobody was around, and then said to Tony, "Take a look in there," and nodded towards the glove box. He looked deadly serious and I knew exactly what he was thinking and I could tell by his expression what he was expecting to find in there. And he opened the glove box really slowly and reached in and put his hand inside - and pulled out the massive rubber dildo!

He didn't know what to make of it. His expression was blank. Totally perplexed! And so as he's sat there gawping down at his hand - that had a fifteen inch rubber cock in it - I put my hand on his thigh and said to him, "Do you fancy a bit of fun before we go to the fight?"

Mick burst out laughing and Tony said, "You fucking dickhead! I thought it was a gun you had in there!"

I knew that was what he'd be thinking, and the reason for him thinking it might have been a gun - not that in a million years I would've been in possession of one - was because Chris (Little) had been shot dead in a gangland hit a few years previously. And more recently, just a few months earlier, someone else we knew very well, 'Barny, David Barnshaw, who was a close associate of Chris, had also been executed. Although he hadn't been shot like Chris had. He'd been kidnapped, doused in petrol - and forced to drink it - and burnt alive. And there were rumours going around that others who were close to Chris, which me and Tony both were, were on a 'hit list'. There was also another (ludicrous) rumour going around that Barny's murder was a warning to me personally. And the supposed reason for it being a warning to me was because the date Barny was murdered was my birthday. Christ knows who started that one, or why. It was just coincidence. Though hearing of Barny's death, along with the rumour, wasn't the best news to get on my birthday I must admit.

I liked Barny. I got on with him, I thought he was alright. But I knew that the rumour would be utter nonsense. Just like the other rumours about there being a hit list were probably nonsense too. Though I believe there was one person who was absolutely kacking themselves because he thought he was next. And he may well have been. Not surprisingly he vanished very quickly and went into hiding.

I took the rumours with a pinch of salt. Not because I was trying to be bravado about it or because I was trying to pretend I wasn't bothered, or had the attitude 'it won't happen to me'. If it was going to happen it would have happened. But I took the rumours with a pinch of salt because there was no reason *for it* to happen to me. I may well have been one of Chris's best mates and done a lot of things with him but unlike others I didn't take liberties with people. I didn't walk onto car pitches and take cars off car dealers like some did - and then take them back three months later and say they were a load of shite, after running them into the ground, and demand another one. I didn't blackmail people. I didn't extort money off people. I didn't take drugs off people. (I didn't take drugs full stop. Or had any involvement with them.) I didn't threaten people or bully and intimidate people. And I didn't barge to the front of queues at pubs and clubs around the town and tell the doormen I was coming in for nothing. I didn't have to actually because I knew most of the doormen and I got on with them and they'd let me in for nothing anyway. And I never once dropped Chris's name, ever, either to gain from or to get me out of a situation. But other people did do things like that (they did worse things too) and they used Chris's name to do them. (And by doing so they probably contributed to him getting shot.)

So there was no real reason really for Tony to think he was going to pull out a gun when he opened the glove box, though I can understand why he did think that. Though bizarrely, not long after that we had a run in with the person accused of the murders of Chris and Barny. And a few years later the same person was accused of a third 'gangland' murder. He was acquitted of all three.

The run in we had with him came about when Tony was working on the door at a pub called The Puss In Boots. I went up to see him one night when he was working there, it was a Wednesday night and as soon as I went in I could sense there was an 'atmosphere'. It was always packed on a Wednesday night at 'The Puss'. They used to have Karaoke on in there which used to draw the crowds in, and when I walked in I noticed a group of about twenty lads stood at the bar. And when I went up to the bar to get served they just stood there and didn't move. One of them, who was stood side on to me, just turned his head and looked at me, arrogantly, then turned back again and carried on talking to his mates and didn't budge. Most people would've said, "Do you want to get served? There you go mate," and stepped aside. But he didn't. He just ignored me. So I barged in-between him and the lad he was talking to and he said, "Oi! What's YOUR fucking game?" So I said, "Well move out of the fucking way then. You could see I wanted to get served." And he looked at me for a second or two and then moved - about two inches! So I got served and I went over to Tony and I said to him, "You'll be earning your money tonight," and he said, "You mean them lot?" and looked at the lads stood at the bar and said, "Yeah, I know I will."

Tony was working with his mate and there were about a dozen of us talking to them both near the entrance. It was a nice summer's night, July time, so a little bit later on we went and sat outside on one of the benches. The lads who were at the bar earlier were also sat outside by now and one of them came and sat right in the middle of us and said to another Tony who was with us, "What's the problem?" So Tony said, "What are you on about? I haven't got a problem." So the lad said, "Yes you have. I think you've got a problem with me." So Tony said, "Well you're wrong. I haven't got a problem with you. I'm just having a drink with my mates."

To be honest it wouldn't have mattered what Tony would've said to him. He could've said, "Sorry," - not that there was anything to say sorry for because he hadn't done anything, or he could've said, "I don't want any trouble." He could've even have offered to have bought the lad and all of his mate's their beer all night but it'd have made no difference because the lad and his mates wanted trouble. So when the lad replied to Tony, "You've been looking at me all night," Tony didn't bother saying anything else. He just butted him in the face! And the fuse was lit! It went off proper.

Fists flew. Pint pots flew. The wooden benches that we were sat at got launched. Stools and chairs got launched - and smashed over people's heads! The pub windows got smashed. A couple of cars on the car park got their windows smashed. They even ripped the metal street signs out of the ground, the 'No Entry' and 'One Way' type signs, and used the steel poles as weapons! And they hurled bricks and rocks and anything else they could get their hands on. It was mental. And then after they'd wrecked the place they fucked off! However we didn't know that they were 'connected' to the man who'd been accused of murdering Chris and Barny - 'Mr A' (as I've been asked to refer to him as) - and they went and told him that *we'd* attacked *them*! For no reason! And about an hour later as we were all stood in the foyer of the pub a car pulled up and the lad who'd started it, the one who Tony butted, got out, and with him was Mr A and another lad.

The car was a BMW and it belonged to Mr A and sometime later I found out something quite interesting about it - it was bomb proof and bullet proof. Someone also said that it used to belong to John Magnier the Irish business magnate and thoroughbred Stud owner who was once a major shareholder in Manchester United.

When Mr A got out of the car I saw him put something in his jacket pocket but I didn't see what it was and then someone who was stood with us shouted, "He's got a gun!" and everyone, quite sensibly, scattered! Everyone apart from me and Tony that is.

Tony didn't flinch. He just stood there. He had loads of bottle did Tony. I just stood there too. Though I think I just froze to the fucking spot with fear! Tony was wearing fingerless gloves, the ones that weightlifters and bodybuilders sometimes wear. He also had his arm in plaster as he'd broken his wrist a few weeks earlier. And when Mr A came marching towards us with his mate he looked at the gloves Tony had on and said, "Have you got those on for me?" Implying that Tony had them on so he could hit him. Trying to calm the situation I said, "No, he hasn't," but no sooner had I said it Tony swung a punch at his mate who was stood near him. But he didn't quite connect. It didn't help with his arm being in plaster, and if he would've connected he'd have probably knocked the lad out because Tony was a very good boxer. And so the lad threw a punch back and as he did Mr A went to put his hand in his jacket pocket.

Now bearing in mind he was the suspect for shooting Chris and he was also a suspect in the murder of Barny, and there were rumours circulating I was on his 'hit list', and add to that someone had just shouted that they'd seen him put a gun in the pocket he was reaching into, you could say I was ever so slightly nervous!

My first thought was to grab the gun so I ran at him and grabbed hold of him around his waist with both of my arms and ran him against the wall where we ended up grappling with each other. And as we were wrestling with each other I felt this almighty whack on the back of my head - his mate had hit me with a cosh. My knees went weak and I felt all dazed and lightheaded and everything went blurred for a moment.

It was like everything had gone into slow motion and I felt like I was going to faint and I went all 'lollipy', and I slumped forward on to Mr A. He must have thought I wanted to give him a cuddle! But he wasn't in a cuddling mood and he just pushed me off. He then reached into his jacket pocket and pulled something out but because I was a bit dazed and I couldn't focus properly I couldn't quite see what it was he'd pulled out. I could see that it was about twelve or fifteen inches long with a rounded end and that it was fairly thick but I couldn't see a trigger on it so I thought, "Well at least it's not a gun." And as he started belting me around the head with whatever it was I thought, "I wonder if he's been in my car and got that dildo out of the glove box!" I was praying he hadn't because if the brawl had made it into the local papers the headline might have been, "No One Shoots At The Puss In Boots But Have-A-Go Hero Gets Battered With His Own Dildo!" which would've been a bit embarrassing for me!

But it wasn't a gun or a dildo that he was battering me senseless with, it was a metal bat (which I later found out he called his 'equaliser') He didn't just hit me the once with it either, he hit me about fifteen times with it!

When the other's who were initially stood with me and Tony - who scattered when they thought Mr A had a gun - saw that it wasn't a gun they came running back, which wasn't a very good idea on their part because Mr A starting laying into them with his bat as well! The three of them eventually left, smashing the remaining unbroken windows as they did so, and a little while later the police arrived. The place was wrecked. And I was standing there covered from head to toe in blood. And when one of the copper's asked Tony what had gone on he said, "Nothing. It's been pretty quiet tonight!"

Obviously we weren't going to assist them with their enquiries. You just don't, do you.

The police knew they were wasting their time even though it was plain to see something *had* gone on, or rather, had gone off. It looked like a bomb had gone off! Oddly enough if a bomb had have gone off Mr A's BMW would've remained intact! The police had already stopped his car up the road. Not that they could get him and his mate out of it as they didn't have any bazookas with them to blow it open with! So Mr A opened the door and they got out and they arrested them, but even though they found a couple of bats in the car that were splattered in my blood they weren't charged as we didn't make a complaint. Though I was complaining of headaches for a few days afterwards!

Both me and Tony got well and truly leathered - no excuses. Though we were at a slight disadvantage seeing as how Tony only had the one arm he could use and we didn't have any metal bats - or rubber dildo's - to fight back with! But what goes around comes around and the lad who started it all got his comeuppance not long after when he did a similar thing at a nightclub in the town.

Mr A had already found out that he'd lied about what went on at the Puss In Boots, which he wasn't too happy about it, and when the lad kicked it off again - and once again expected Mr A to clear up the mess - Mr A took him for a 'little ride' in the back of his car. But ten minutes into the journey Mr A and a friend of his who was with him got a whiff of a foul stench coming from the back seat and when Mr A said, "What the fuck's that smell!!" the lad informed them that he'd shit his pants! The thought of what was going to happen to him quite literally had scared him shitless! And Mr A's car may well have been bomb proof and bullet proof but it wasn't shit proof. And so not wanting his interior splattered with diarrhoea Mr A and his friend kicked the lad out of his car and dumped him at the side of the road where he was left to clear his own mess up for once!

When the truth came out about who had actually caused the trouble that led to me and Tony getting a good hiding Mr A wanted to meet us to apologise. For one reason or another I never met him, though I think Tony did, and it wasn't until around two years later that I finally did meet him.

It was in Master's. The club Paul Madati ran and where Alex Higgins splattered me in snot!

I actually met Alex Higgins many years later at Belle Vue greyhound track. (He loved to gamble on the horses and the dogs.) He didn't remember me and I never mentioned the incident. He had cancer at the time and he didn't look well at all, and I felt really sorry for him looking at him. I had a bit of a chat with him and I asked him if he had any tips. He told me the name of one he fancied in the next race so I stuck a fiver on it and it lost! I said to him that it was a good job he could play snooker because he'd never make a living as a racing tipster, which he found funny. Maybe he did remember me and gave me a duff tip in revenge for me saying what I did to him! My dad also once met Alex Higgins, though at first he thought he was a burglar! It was after my dad had split up with my mum and he was living in a bedsit in a place called Withington. My dad had been in the pub next door, The Turnpike, and when he went home he saw this bloke climbing through the window of the ground floor flat so he ran over and dragged him out and pinned him on the ground, and he got a bit of a shock when he saw it was Alex Higgins! Higgins wasn't trying to break in the flat.

Well he was but not to burgle it. He was seeing the woman who lived there but she was out, so to get in he thought he'd climb through the window. My dad and Higgins had a laugh about it and seeing as how they both liked a drink they went back in the Turnpike and got pissed together!

I used to go in Master's all the time and a couple of years after the incident at the Puss In Boots I was in there one Saturday night. At the end of the night I saw Mr A coming over to say goodbye to Paul who I was sat opposite of at a table with a few others. I'd seen Mr A in there during the course of the night but he hadn't recognised me and so I said to Paul not to say anything to him when he came over. I wasn't avoiding him, I just didn't think there was any point in speaking to him. What happened had happened. It was one of them things and it was over with. But I should've known better than to have said anything to Paul because I knew what he was like for having a wind up. And I could tell by the grin on his face when I said not to say anything that he *would* say something. And he did. The cunt! And when Mr A shook his hand and said goodbye to him - and acknowledged a few others who were sat at the table - Paul said to him, "You know Nick don't you?" and nodded in my direction. And then looked at me and smirked! And I looked him as if to say, "You twat!" Mr A then turned to me, smiled and said, "No, we've not met," and held his hand out. So I said, "We have met actually - the last time we met you smashed my head in with a metal cosh at the Puss In Boots!" He looked a little bit shocked and he said, "So *you're* Nick!" and he said, "I've been wanting to meet you to apologise for what happened that night and to thank you for your discretion you showed towards the police," referring to us not saying anything to the police about what had happened. And fair play to him, he apologised.

He was in a bit of a rush. He said he was off to an Indian restaurant up the road to meet some people, and said for me and my mate, Mark, who I was with, to go up there because he wanted to have a bit of chat, not particularly about what had happened at the Puss In Boots but also about some of the stories that were circulating. And we shook hands and he left.

I was in two minds whether to go or not but Mark said, "We may as well go." So I said to him, "What, to see what he's got to say and clear the air and get it all sorted?" And then said, "Yeah, I suppose you're right." And Mark said, "No. I couldn't give a fuck about all that bollocks. I just fancy a curry!"

So we went. But when we got there it was packed and we were stood waiting for a good ten minutes. I could see Mr A sat at the far side of the room. He was sat with about six others and it looked like he was in deep conversation, so I thought well I'm not going to go over and say, "I'm here! What do you want?!" So I said to Mark, "Come on, let's fuck off." But just as we were about to walk out one of the waiters came over and said to me, "Are you Nick?" So I said, "Yes." And he apologised for the wait and took me and Mark to a table - Mr A had seen us both stood there and had told them to sort us out with a table.

So we sat down. And no sooner had we, two pints of Harp lager came over. You remember Harp lager don't you? It was popular then. It tasted fucking horrible but it was popular! And as we took a mouthful of it a plate of

Poppadom's came over. Then ten minutes later two curry's came over - and we'd not even looked at the menu! We'd not even been *given* a menu let alone looked at one and ordered from it!

Mark was loving it! He said, "This is alright innit!" He was wolfing it down! And then not long after, Mr A, who I presumed had sent the food and drinks over, came over and sat down and we had a chat. I can't remember most of what he said because it was one o'clock in the morning by then and I'd been drinking all night and I was half pissed! But at least we had a chat. He then went back to his table and me and Mark got up to leave. And as we stood up I heard the bloke who was sat on the table next to us with his mate say to the waiter, "How long will our food be? We've been waiting nearly three quarters of an hour now and it's still not here." And the waiter gave a bit of a puzzled look and said to him, "I've brought it over haven't I?" And the bloke said, "No. You haven't. And we also ordered two pints of Harp and you've not brought them over either."

I then realised that I'd presumed wrongly; Mr A *hadn't* sent the food and drinks over. The waiter had brought the two bloke's orders to the wrong table and given it to us by mistake. And we'd just eaten it! And swilled it down with their two pints of lager!

'Time for a sharp exit' as the Harp advert used to say that was on television in them days!

At the time I thought that would probably be the only chat I'd be having with Mr A. However it turned out not to be the case. And the next time I spoke to him was to help out a mate, though helping that mate out could've proved very costly for me. Not costly as in physical harm but costly as in financial loss. But, a friend in need, as they say. Is a fucking pain in the arse! And when my friend heard that Mr A wanted a word with him he was sweating a little bit. And *I* still get a cold sweat now when I think about how I nearly lost twenty grand in cash that was owed to Mr A!

My friend was involved in a business deal with someone that went tits up. The other person had put money into the deal and he wanted it back and someone suggested to him that Mr A would be able to do this for him and so he went to see him and they came to an arrangement. To cut a very long story short(ish) someone rang my mate and said that he no longer owed the money to the other person, he now owed it to Mr A and said that it'd be in his best interests to pay up. Immediately. As soon as my mate heard that Mr A was involved he became a bit nervous (like most would) and he rang me and asked me what I thought he should do. So I said the best thing to do would be to meet Mr A and sort it out (something didn't quite stack up with what he'd been told, namely the amount of money he'd been told he owed) and I said I'd arrange a meeting. I didn't have Mr A's number at the time so I rang a mate of mine, Phil, and he arranged a meeting, the upshot being that my friend agreed to pay back a percentage of what was said he owed.

He paid back some of it within a couple of weeks and it left a balance of £20,000, and when he'd got the £20k together he asked me would I take it down to Mr A, which I said I'd do. So one morning I picked up the money, which was all in twenty pound notes in a white A4 envelope, and off I went.

It was a Wednesday and I'd arranged to be at Mr A's office at 10 o'clock. But it'd only just gone nine when I picked the money up so it was a bit too early to go. So I thought I'd nip into the town centre first and have a walk around and kill half an hour. So I drove into Stockport and parked up on the multi-storey car park and had a wander around the shops.

I always do the lottery on a Saturday and on a Wednesday, without fail. I don't know why I bother because I never win but I keep on playing it, like everyone else does, because of the 'chance' that my numbers might just come up, even though the chances of them actually coming up are very slim. In hindsight, when the lottery first came out I should've just had a lucky dip, that way I could've stopped playing it years ago because the numbers would be different every week and I'd never remember them, therefore I'd be none the wiser if they came up. But like most people who play I have fixed numbers, which are 1,2,3,4,5 and 6 - and which probably explains why I've never fucking won! They're not really 1,2,3,4,5 and 6, though would you believe that over 10,000 people do have those numbers as their fixed numbers every week. And so with me knowing what my numbers are off by heart I keep playing. I'm hooked. Just like everyone else who has fixed numbers is hooked. And here's one for you that'll make you realise just how hooked we all are on playing the lottery. If say at ten past two on a Saturday afternoon someone said to you that a horse was running in the 2.30 at Ascot and it was fourteen million to one you wouldn't run to the bookies to put a fiver on it would you? No, you wouldn't. Because you know that if the bookies are offering odds of fourteen million to one then it's got absolutely no chance of winning. But if at ten past seven on a Saturday night you realised that you'd forgotten to put your usual numbers on the lottery you'd leg it to the Co-op at the top of the road to put them on - even though the odds of winning are the same, fourteen million to one! It's ridiculous really when you think about it but we all do it because it's the fear of not putting our numbers on and them coming up that forces us to continuing playing, and we daren't miss. We really are hooked. And fucked! And Camelot, who run the National Lottery *know* we're hooked - and fucked! That's why there was such an outcry when they introduced the Wednesday draw years ago with the same numbers, 1 - 49, as it was then. They could have quite easily used numbers 50 - 99 (as was suggested) but they knew that if they did that not as many people would play. So they kept the numbers at 1 - 49 knowing that most people used the same fixed numbers every Saturday and in the back of people's minds they'd think that they'd better play on Wednesday as well using the same numbers just in case they came up. Clever, eh! Greedy, but clever.

So after I'd had a mooch around the shops I went in WH Smith's and put the lottery on. I filled out the slip, three lines as usual, and gave it to the girl behind the counter and put my hand in my pocket to get three quid out (it was only a £1 to play at the time.) But all I pulled out was a pound coin and I thought, "Oh bollocks! I haven't got enough money on me." I then thought, "Well that's odd. I could've sworn I had twenty grand this morning!"

I then realised what I'd done. And boy did I panic!

When I'd picked up the money that morning, when I got back to my car I opened the rear door and threw it on the back seat. Well where else could I have put it? I couldn't have put it in the glove box could I? There was no room. Because there was a fucking huge dildo in there! And when I parked up on the multi-storey car park I'd just forgotten all about it and walked off and left it lying on the back seat in full view!

I remember standing in WH Smiths and a cold sweat coming over me and it felt like I'd gone into a trance. It was like I was in a dream, a bad one - one that could well have turned into a nightmare for me - and when the girl behind the counter said to me, "That's three pounds please," I just looked at her and said, "Fucking Hell!" and ran out!

She must have thought, "Well it's not free you fucking idiot!"

I was parked on the top level of the car park and as I was legging it up the stairs, at the top of each flight was a sign that said, "Have You Locked Your Car?" And I started panicking even more because I didn't remember doing it! And when I got to the top level and ran out onto the car park and looked over at my car I realised I hadn't locked it because I could see that the rear door was open by about an inch.

Then I didn't just panic, I felt like throwing myself off the top of the multi-storey!

I was about fifty yards away from my car and I stopped running. I just stood and looked at the rear door and thought, "It's gone. What the fuck am I going to do?" So I just strolled over to my car, shaking my head thinking, "You silly bastard!" But when I got to my car and opened the back door I saw that the envelope was still on the back seat!

Oh what relief!

The reason the rear door was slightly open was because after I'd flung the envelope on the back seat I hadn't shut it properly. I'd also been having a bit of a problem with the electronics on my car and one or two things weren't working on it. The central locking wasn't working and neither were the warning lights and the 'ping' noises that tell you that the doors aren't closed properly. So I'd actually driven from where I'd collected the money from to the town centre with the door open. It could've easily fell out on the way! Imagine walking down the road and finding an envelope with £20k in it. You wouldn't need to play the lottery would you! Though no doubt that if any of you *would* have found it you'd have gone straight to the police station with it and handed it in wouldn't you?

Like fuck you would!

Neither my friend nor Mr A ever knew about that mishap. Though no doubt some fucker will tell them after they've read this book!

The term MILF denotes a sexually attractive older woman, generally aged between 30 and 50, and with me being in that age bracket - and being sexually attractive - (that sounds rather vain and conceited I know, but I am) it'd be fair of people, usually younger men, to class me as a MILF. However as well as being seen as a MILF by younger men I'm also seen as a 'Cougar' by my friends.

A Cougar is typically defined as a woman that's aged over 40 and who sexually pursues younger men and because that's what I (unashamedly) do my friends refer to me as one. And they love hearing me telling them all about my exploits! Although my exploits have also caused me to lose friends, which to be honest saddens me. And I lost one very good friend which saddened me a great deal. (To this day she still thinks I slept with her son, which I didn't. Though I did sleep with two of his friends – at the same time.)

Ever since 'Cougar' Mrs Robinson, the older married woman played by Anne Bancroft who seduced the naive young Benjamin (Dustin Hoffman) in the film The Graduate all those years ago, the idea of older women having relationships with younger men in order to fulfil their sexual needs and desires has been a popular subject, and in hit television series such as Desperate Housewives, Sex And The City and Cougar Town older mature women were seen taking control of their sex lives.

Middle aged women in particular could relate to television shows such as these which was why they were hugely popular. In real life however some women are a little less certain about the merits of being dubbed a Cougar. For example the Cougars in shows such as Sex And The City and Desperate Housewives are portrayed as confident, assertive middle aged women who are empowering and who promote a sense of self-worth. But quite often in real life, Cougars like myself aren't seen as assertive and empowering we're seen as predators! You could even say it's condescending to be called a Cougar, though I'd much rather be called a Cougar than a dirty old slapper as one of my friends jokingly calls me!

But even though my friend is only joking when she calls me a dirty old slapper she's probably not far off the mark. I'm no shrinking violet that's for sure. And neither am I ashamed at my behaviour and some of the things I do. On the outside I'm a seemingly dignified, respectful, elegant woman. In reality though I'm deviant, vulgar and sexual immoral. Well according to some of my friends I am!

But I'm not alone. There are several "sexually immoral" women like me in the vicinity whom I know very well. And I dare say there'll be quite a few others too in the locality who I don't know, just like there'll be in any suburb in Britain. We're not a group of sad, lonely, divorced (and in one case married) women who trawl the bars of Wilmslow and the surrounding areas on the prowl for young men to drag back home for sex - though on occasions me and one of my friends do do that! My friend does it quite often actually and she's married! Though she does have her husband's approval.

Her husband encourages her to do it too. And not just with young men. He's quite happy for her to sleep with any man she chooses regardless of their age - on the condition she tells him all about it, in graphic detail, afterwards. He gets a kick out of it. He also gets a kick out of watching her having sex with other men. Sometimes two or three men at the same time, although that's always pre-arranged as opposed to his wife picking up strangers in a bar and taking them home.

As I say, we're not a group of lonely women who are continually on the hunt for young males, although we are part of a group. A swingers group. And it'll be a surprise to 99.9% of the residents of Wilmslow and Cheshire to learn that once a month one of the biggest sex parties in the swinger fraternity takes place here and invited couples from all over the UK come to it. And you'd be surprised who turns up. I don't know how true this is because I didn't attend this particular party but by all accounts a certain 'housewife' of Cheshire and one of her friends once turned up at one of the parties - although they didn't participate. Well as far as I know they didn't!

Apparently she's a friend of the hosts and she and her friend turned up for 'research purposes.' Though I don't recall any swingers parties ever being shown on the RHOCH! Though oddly enough - and it may well be just a coincidence - there was a scene in one of the episodes of The Real Housewives" that looked like it had come straight out of one of the parties. I forget which of the wives it was who had the party but she had two muscular young men who were bare-chested and wearing a dickie bow and trousers welcoming guests and offering them champagne.

Guests at the swinger parties are greeted in a similar fashion as they too are welcomed by two bare-chested muscular young men wearing dickie bow ties. The only difference is they haven't got any trousers on! They offer more than champagne too – they offer themselves. And I once took them both up on their offer! Unfortunately this was what caused the rift between me and my former best friend who accused me of sleeping with her son. (Neither of the two young men were her son, though they were friends of his.)

The parties are like any other swinger's house party, of which there are dozens and dozens every weekend in houses the length and breadth of Britain. Although this one takes place in slightly more opulent and luxurious surroundings than your average swingers house party. But the concept is the same; you see someone, or a couple, who takes your fancy and off you pop to the bedroom with them. Or just get down to it on the living room floor in front of everyone! Though there is one rule at the parties: *you can pick and choose but you can't refuse.* In other words if someone approaches you who you aren't particularly attracted to you can't say no, and that's made clear on the invitation. Though take my word for it, you wouldn't turn *anyone* down at this couple's party!

Sometimes though the choice of who you (initially) partner with is made for you in a fun way by playing a game of open the box. The couple who host the party have had one of the bookshelves in their house split into a number of small wooden compartments each of which has a little door on it which is locked, and inside each compartment is a piece of paper with a number written on it, from 1 – 30 say, depending on how many people/couples are there. (At one party the numbers were from 1 – 60. It was more like a Roman Orgy than a swinger's get together!)

Half of the guests are given another piece of paper with one of the corresponding numbers written on it. The other half of the guests are then given a key and they'll open one of the compartments and take out the piece of paper and shout out the number that's on it and whoever has got the piece of paper with that number is their initial partner(s). I say their *initial* partner because after that it's a free for all and you can go with whoever takes your fancy.

'You never know what goes on behind closed doors' as the saying goes and people would be quite shocked if they knew what goes on behind some of the doors of the houses around the Wilmslow area. They'd probably quite like to join in too!

As for being labelled a Cougar. Do I take it as a compliment or an insult? Well in truth, neither. While some women - not dissimilar to those in Desperate Housewives and Sex And The City - may proudly call themselves Cougars, possibly as a way of showing their self-confidence and asserting their independence, ultimately it is just a label. A stereotype. There are lots of attractive middle aged women like me. The only difference is most of them don't jump into bed with younger men half their age at the first chance they get! But I'm not a middle aged woman who yearns to be a twenty year old girl again, I'm an adult who seeks fun with young men. What's wrong with that? Why should being a stereotype stop me from having fun and control who I choose to date and have sex with? And if you're seen as a Cougar yourself and you sometimes doubt whether you should stop 'hunting', my advice to you is carry on.

Younger men have far less emotional baggage. They have far more energy too!

What would you consider the more serious offence; a house burglary in a working class area or a flyer promoting a book being put through the letter box of a house in an upper class area? The answer, obviously, is a house burglary in a working class area - though Greater Manchester Police think differently. And out of those two 'offences' – the latter of which 99.9% of people *wouldn't* class as an offence – which do you think requires a more speedy response by the police? Again, the house burglary is the answer. But yet again Greater Manchester Police think differently. They think that a flyer being posted through the letter box of a house in an upper class area warrants a more speedy response.

Within 24 hours to be exact.

I recently released a revised edition of a previous book I did and out of courtesy I contacted all those whose stories are in the book to tell them I was doing so. Some replied some didn't. One of those who did reply was a fella called Joe who lives in Sheffield. His story was titled Dear Jeremy Corbyn, Jo Swinson, Gina Miller, Tony Blair And The Like. It was about Brexit and how people tried to overturn the result and stop Brexit from happening. Joe voted leave and in his story, or letter as he called it, he talks about illegal immigrants flocking to the UK, which was the main reason people voted leave. Joe asked me if he could add a few things to his story so I said yes and told him to email them to me and I'd stick them in for him. He also asked if he could change the title of his story so I said yes, no problem, and asked him what he wanted it changing to and he said, "I want to call it The More Illegal Immigrants That Drown In The Channel The

Better – People Are Sick To Death Of Them Coming Here."

I thought, "Fuck Me! That's a bit strong! I'm sick to death of them coming here too, like most people are, but I wouldn't wish for them to drown in the English Channel. Send them to Rwanda when they get here by all means. But it's a bit much wishing for them to drown trying to get here."

And so I suggested to Joe that he keep the same title or use a different one but he was adamant he wanted that one. So I thought well it's his story and if that's what he wants to call it it's his choice.

Not far from where I live is a place called Hale, in Cheshire. It's a very posh area and there were plans to house over a hundred asylum seekers in a hotel in the centre of the village which the locals weren't too happy about. Now even though I thought Joe's new title was a bit harsh, from a publicity point of view it was gold. It's an attention grabber. So I had over 2,500 flyers printed and used his story along with the title of it to publicise my book. And that's the ONLY reason I used it – to publicise the book. And I posted the flyers around Hale. As I was posting the leaflets quite a few people, locals, stopped me and asked about the book saying it looked very interesting and that they were going to buy it. They were very friendly and polite and I stood and chatted with some of them for a few minutes. However someone else stopped me too, a woman, though she wasn't friendly or polite. She was just fucking rude and ill-mannered. She'd come out of a house on a road called West Gate and she was the passenger in a car and she had one of the flyer's in her hand and she wound the window down and said, "It's disgusting wishing people should drown. You shouldn't be putting these through people's letter boxes. I'm going to the police." So I said to her, "Hang on a minute. Let me explain. It's not my story. I only published the book...." But as I was talking she wound the car window up and motioned to me with her hand to go away. So I motioned back to her with my hand for her to wind the window down, and mouthed, "Put your window down please – I'll explain," (In hindsight I should've just motioned with two fingers telling her to fuck off!) She did wind her window down, very briefly, but as I started to talk she interrupted and cut me off and in a raised voice she said, "I'm NOT interested. Go away. You're disgusting. I'm going to the police with this," and shooed me away with her hand again and wound the window up and they drove off. I thought, "Oh fuck off you stupid stuck up bitch!" (And the bloke that was driving was a prick too, wittering on with himself) and I didn't think any more of it and carried on posting the flyers. I wasn't bothered in the slightest about her going to the police because in my eyes I hadn't done anything wrong. All I'd done was use extracts from a story in the book - a story that wasn't mine - to promote my book. Albeit the story had a title that I suppose you could describe as controversial. But I'd even put on the flyer that some people may find the title of Joe's story distasteful. However even though *I* thought I hadn't done anything wrong the police thought differently and the following day at around half eight on a Sunday morning nearly half a dozen coppers turned up at my house in two cars and a police van and arrested me for a public order offence (without elaborating on exactly what the offence was.) The upshot being that I was lobbed in the back of the van and taken to a police station the other side of Manchester in Pendleton in Salford, and after spending ten hours (yes, TEN fucking hours!) in a cell I was interviewed and released on bail pending a decision by the Crown Prosecution Service as whether to proceed with charges or not.

At the end of the interview I was asked by one of coppers if there was anything I'd like to add and so I said yes and said, "If that extract was published in a national newspaper such as The Daily Mail or The Sun and a complaint was made would you go and arrest the editor of the newspaper? No, you wouldn't, would you?"

And it's true. They wouldn't.

Likewise, if the book had been published by one of the big publishing houses such as Penguin books and a famous author had written it would the police have gone and arrested the CEO of Penguin books and arrested the author? No, they wouldn't have. Yet because I'm a relatively unknown writer who self publishes and I live in the area, the police come to my house, team handed, and arrest me.

Everyone I've spoken to about my arrest says the same thing; it's a load of bollocks. And I've written to the CPS and told them exactly that. This is part of the letter I wrote:

I was arrested on the above date and you're currently looking at whether to bring charges or not and although you have my statement which I made to the police I also wish to provide you with further information for you to consider, which, hopefully, after reading it, along with my statement, you'll agree that no charges should be brought against me. I wasn't told what specific section of the public order offence it is that I was arrested for and I don't remember it being stated during the interview either, though I think I heard 'publication' being said prior to the interview commencing. I've tried contacting the O.I.C (Officer In Charge) or rather, Obnoxious Ignorant Cunt, numerous times and left messages and sent emails asking for him to contact me for clarification but I've received no reply. So I've had to Google what section I think it relates to and I think the section may possibly be possession / publication / distribution of inflammatory material intending to stir up racial hatred and anti immigrant feeling. Apologies for repeating myself as I've said some of this in my statement but my arrest is a load of bollocks. Complete and utter fucking bollocks. I'm also highly fucking pissed off and extremely annoyed about the manner in which I was arrested. Having read the possession/publication part of the public order section on Google I'm guessing that your decision to bring charges is based on whether or not my intention was to stir up racial/religious hatred. Well I can tell you now, it wasn't. The only thing I intended to stir up was publicity for my book – like I've done countless times in the past using similar marketing methods in other areas (see enclosed marketing material.) If I wanted to stir up racial tensions why the hell would I go to Hale - one of the poshest parts of Cheshire - to do it? What was I hoping that the wealthy, posh, well heeled, 'nasty, vicious, middle aged thugs' of Hale do? Get tanked up on Dom Perignon in Piccolino's one lunch time and then charge around to the asylum seekers hotel and hit them with their Guggi handbags and spray Giorgio Armani perfume in their eyes? It's pathetic, absolutely fucking pathetic. And that woman who complained is pathetic too. Like numerous people have commented on Facebook about this, some people really have got nothing better to do. Any normal person would have just thought "what a load of shite" and flung the flyer in the bin. Not run to the police with it. And apart from the fact there wasn't any asylum seekers in Hale when I was posting the leaflets - and may not be if resident protest groups get their way - if I really wanted to stir up racial tensions I wouldn't go to Hale to do it would I? I'd go to one of the many inner city areas across England where racial tensions ARE high such as the area in Sheffield that Joe mentions in his story where there are hundreds of immigrants already living there and distribute the flyer's there. It's ludicrous - laughable even - to think that my intention was to stir up racial hatred. And I certainly wouldn't have received a letter off Prince William about the book in question if he or his advisors, who would have read the book to check through it, thought that I was in any way racist or if there was anything inciting racial hatred in it. I also wouldn't receive messages and cards from black/mixed race premiership football managers like Chris Hughton wishing me good luck with my books if I was a racist would I? (Copy enclosed.) And if I thought for one minute that I might be committing an offence by distributing the flyers and there was a possibility that I could get arrested for stirring up racial hatred by doing so the last place I'd have sent one of the flyers would have been to Altrincham fucking police station! (See enclosed)...

As yet I've received no reply. Altrincham police station covers Hale by the way. But what pissed me off, and really annoyed me, was the manner in which I was arrested. *I get arrested because some woman, who comes from a posh part of Cheshire, makes a ridiculous complaint about having a promotional leaflet for a book shoved through her letter box and the police act upon it immediately and send nearly half a dozen coppers out within 24 hours to make an arrest. And I get lobbed in the back of a police van and carted off to a police station eleven miles away and get locked in a cell for ten fucking hours. Yet when someone like a pal of mine gets his house burgled in Reddish where I live, which *isn't* a posh area, like he did a couple of weeks previously and reported it to the police it took the police EIGHT days to come out to investigate it. As I put at the beginning of this story, what's more serious; a house burglary in a working class area or a flyer being put through the letter box of a house in an upper class area? Obviously the police think the latter. And only two days before my arrest a builder at the top of my road had his van broken into and had over £3,000 worth of tools nicked out of it and when he rang the police they said it was 'only' a car crime and they wouldn't be sending anybody out and just gave him a crime reference number and told him to ring his insurance company.

What kind of policing is that?

It comes across as though the police have the attitude that if you're 'well to do' and live in a posh area they'll investigate a crime for you - no matter how petty the complaint is. But if you're an 'ordinary Joe' who lives in an ordinary suburb they *won't* investigate a crime for you but they'll speedily rush to such an area, within 24hrs, team handed, to nick you for something, even if it's a ridiculous, and false accusation. Furthermore, the police were quick to march through my front door to arrest me but when I tried contacting them to explain exactly *why* they marched through my front door they couldn't be arsed replying. And the police wonder why they come in for so much stick?

Also, as I pointed out in my letter to the CPS, there's no need for me to stir up anti immigrant feeling because the majority of Britain *already has* anti immigrant feeling. And the people of Hale have all got anti immigrant feeling too otherwise they wouldn't be protesting about having immigrants housed there!

My arrest really is a load of fucking bollocks. There was no need whatsoever for the police to turn up mob handed at my house early on a Sunday morning. They could've just sent one, or maybe two coppers to ask my side of the story without arresting me and it could've all been cleared up. It's a sad state of affairs when the police respond within a day to a complaint about a flyer but take over a week to respond to a house burglary - and just don't respond at all to car crime.

But the saddest thing of all about my arrest was that it left my youngest daughter deeply disappointed. Not disappointed with *me* for getting arrested. She thought that was fucking hilarious! It was a *consequence* of my arrest that left her feeling disappointed. It also left me and my wife feeling disappointed for her too.

Me, my wife and my two daughters regularly go to Hale walking our dog. There's a restaurant in Hale Village, I forget the name of it now, and whenever we go my youngest says she'd like to go there one day. It's a bit out of my price bracket to be honest! However it was my daughter's 16th birthday at the end of January, three weeks after my arrest. And prior to my arrest, seeing as how sixteen is a 'special' birthday, I'd told her that we'd go there for her birthday which she was over the moon about. But we couldn't go because my bail conditions prevented me from going into Hale. That's another reason why I was so pissed off and annoyed with my fucking pathetic arrest, an arrest that was instigated by a fucking pathetic old busybody. But, as always, as those of you who have read my books know, I always try and see the funny side of things. And although I didn't think that my arrest was very funny there is a slightly humorous side to this story.

The night before I was arrested I was watching one of those 24 hours in police custody type programmes and it showed the police smashing down the front door of a house and arresting the bloke whose house it was. My youngest was sat watching it with me. She knows that I've got a bit of a 'chequered' past and that I've been in prison and as the coppers handcuffed the bloke and put him in the back of the police van she jokingly said, "That's you dad!" So I laughed and said, "I don't think so. The days of *me* getting arrested are long gone." Then fuck me, the following morning the police turn up at our house and arrest me! And when I came back home later that night and walked in the front door my daughter came out of her bedroom, leant over the banister and with a wry smile on her face said to me, "What was you saying about those days being long gone Dad?!"

During the Brexit debate, which turned into an utter fiasco and made the UK the laughing stock of Europe, I wrote what I suppose you could call an 'open letter' for everyone to read and I uploaded it to the internet. It was directed at those who were doing their utmost to stop Brexit, in the main, Jeremy Corbyn, Jo Swinson, Gina, Miller and Tony Blair.

I'm not massive into politics. I just felt like getting something off my chest. Some will agree with what I wrote, others won't. I don't really care to be honest. But I do care about what's happening to this country. And like millions of others, and like I put in my letter, I'm sick to death of immigrants flooding here - which was the reason people voted leave - and turning this country into a shit hole.

Right now, people who were born and bred in Britain and who have lived here all their lives and who have contributed to this country and paid all their taxes and national insurance contributions are struggling to pay for the basics. They're struggling to buy food. They're struggling to clothe their kids. They're struggling to pay their gas and electric bills and struggling to pay their rent and mortgage, and thousands are relying on foodbanks, whilst immigrants get it all for free and get put up in hotels and in private accommodation.

It cost me and my family over £200 a night to stay in a hotel on a short break in London not so long ago. How much does it cost an asylum seeker to stay in a hotel? Nothing. In fact, THEY GET PAID to stay in a hotel, £49.18 a week, each. Extra if they have children. Female asylum seekers also get a one off payment of £300 if they're expecting. (I don't recall my wife getting £300 payments for our two sons when they were born.) And they get fed three meals a day, plus free prescriptions, free dental care, and free eye tests (and free glasses if need be) whereas the likes of me and nearly every other British citizen has to pay for it.

Is it any wonder asylum seekers flock here in their thousands? And will KEEP ON flocking here. And is it any wonder that millions of us are fed up and extremely pissed off about it?

The worst thing that a lot of politicians did was oppose the Rwanda bill. Even royalty and the Church of England got in on the act to try and stop it. Prince Charles - or King Charles as he is now - said it was "appalling" that illegal immigrants should be deported to Rwanda. But how many immigrants has he got living on *his* street? None, is the answer. If he's so in favour of immigrants coming here why not put a few hundred up in Balmoral and Sandringham and in the dozens of other royal residences that the royal family have around Britain? He could house thousands of them. (And he'd soon change his tune if he did and found out what it's like to have them living on his doorstep.)

The same goes for the Church of England. Let immigrants stay in their churches if they care for them so much. The Church of England is worth millions. They too could easily afford to house a few thousand of them. Have they? No. But, as it's been widely reported on they'll happily baptise asylum seekers - the vast majority of which come from Muslim countries - converting them to Christianity in order for them to claim that they are at risk of persecution if they are deported back to their home country due to their 'new found' religion. (A religion that most of them are opposed to and couldn't give a shit about.)

And the same goes for those two-faced hypocritical Hope not Hate and 'Refugees Welcome' protesters. How many of them have offered to house an immigrant? None of them. Well, apart from Gary Lineker that is. (And the one that stayed at his house would've been handpicked too. It certainly wouldn't have been one that was plucked out of a dinghy off a beach in Dover that's for sure.)

When these placard waving do-gooders see another boat full of (healthy fighting age male) asylum seekers arrive here do they actually think, "Oh, wonderful! More!" Nonsense. It's all for show:

"Look at *me*. How good am I! Doing my bit."

But when they get the opportunity to do their bit, they won't.

Watch the YouTube video of the guy pretending to be from a refugee charity who asked fifty of the 'Hope Not Haters' at a protest would they be willing to house a refugee, having first 'drawn them in' by asking them about the kind of house they lived in and how many spare bedrooms they had. Each one he asked said they had at least one spare bedroom, many had two, but not one of them said they'd be willing to accommodate a refugee. And when he asked them would they like to sponsor a refugee for £50, just a £1 a week, instead of housing one, they all said no thanks. And when he asked them would they be willing for a refugee to come to their house for a couple of hours each week for a 'chat and a cup of tea' to help them settle in and to make them feel welcome in Britain, guess what every single one of them said? No! Their excuses being that they "didn't really have the time." Yet they've got plenty of time to spend at 'Anti Fascist' and 'Far Right' protests waving 'Refugees Welcome' placards.

Refugees Welcome? Don't make me laugh you fucking hypocrites.

The majority of people thought the idea to send illegal immigrants to Rwanda was a good one. Help the genuine ones, yes. The one's that *really are* fleeing persecution and war. But get rid of the rest; the ones that are here for a free ride.

You've only got to look at the pictures in the newspapers and watch the news reports on television to see that nearly all the 'refugees' coming here who say that they are "scared for their lives" in their own country and are "fleeing persecution" are fit and healthy young males aged around 18 - 25. Very few are women, kids or the elderly. These 'refugees' are liars. They are *not* fleeing persecution. And they are *not* genuine refugees. And anyone who believes that they are - King Charles and the leaders of the Church of England included (and football pundits) - are fucking idiots.

You don't see many fit and healthy 18 - 25 year old Ukrainian males trying to sneak into Britain do you? That's because they've decided to stay and fight for their country, a fight which is against one of the most powerful armies in the world, Russia. Unlike those seeking refuge in our country who all they are (supposedly) fleeing are rag tag bands of rebels and half-baked piss pot armies.

One other thing that amazes me about these "poor helpless refugees" who sneak into our country is that on the way here they always seem to lose their passports and ID papers and anything else that may reveal their identity, their (true) age, their origin and so on. But they never lose their mobile phones do they? Isn't that amazing?

Those who try and cross the channel in dinghies and small boats know the risks, so if they drown trying to get here it's their own fault and they've got no-one to blame but themselves. If you cross a busy main road when the lights are on green instead of waiting for them to turn red and you get knocked down it's your own fault isn't it? And the same goes for illegal immigrants. They're not being forced at gunpoint to get in those boats are they?

I've got no sympathy for them. And I'm not alone either. Many others think the same way. There was a group of us talking about the immigration problem/Rwanda plan in our local pub not so long ago - a pub that's not far from an area in Sheffield that's blighted by immigrants - and one bloke in our company said that when he sees on television that a boat has capsized in the English Channel and immigrants have drowned he doesn't think, "Oh, how sad." He said he thinks, "Good. I hope more boats capsize."

A couple of years ago the brother of an illegal immigrant who drowned in the channel was interviewed on television and he actually said that his brother wasn't in any danger in the country where he lived and that he was only coming to England because he wanted a better life. (And quite unbelievably his family and the other families of those who drowned tried to sue UK Coastguards saying it was their fault.) Well I wouldn't mind a better life myself. And I dare say that millions of other British people wouldn't mind a better life as well.

I wouldn't mind going to live in Spain and if I drowned in the Med' off the coast of Benidorm trying to get there would I - or my family - get any sympathy off the Spanish people? No. And if I made it to Spain would I be allowed to stay there? No, I wouldn't. I'd be sent back. Just like the illegal immigrants who try to get into our country should be sent back - or sent to Rwanda.

And that's the key word: *illegal*.

If you do something that's illegal you're breaking the law - you're committing a criminal act. (And a lot of the immigrants ARE criminals, coming from places like Albania - where there is no war or persecution. In actual fact Albania is a popular holiday destination.) And if a UK Citizen like myself were to break the law and commit criminal acts would I be rewarded for doing so by being put up in a cushy hotel and given three meals a day and have all my bills paid for AND be given nearly a £50 a week spending allowance? No, I certainly wouldn't. I'd be flung in a police cell.

Some people, i.e. out of touch MP's and those who have no immigration problem in the 'nice' areas where they live, have got no idea of just how much the majority of the UK resent illegal immigrants. And just because people protest about immigration it doesn't make us racists or fascists or 'Far Right' as we're branded. We're just fed up with immigrants flooding here and claiming benefits, free housing, free health care and anything else they can get their hands on whilst some of our own citizens - some of whom have fought for this country - get nothing and are left homeless and are forced to beg on the streets.

It's not right. Or fair.

The answer to stopping illegal immigrants coming here by the way is simple: give them nothing when they get here. Obviously preventing them from getting here in the first place is the best way to do it (and giving ££millions to African countries to try and stop it isn't the answer) but if they do get here, give them sod all. Ex-servicemen who have fought for this country and who are now sleeping rough on the streets are given sod all so why give an illegal immigrant anything?

Like I say, nearly all of those who come here aren't in danger or in fear for their lives in the country they've "escaped" from like they claim they are. They just use that as an excuse. But let's assume that *is* the reason for them fleeing their country. If so, once they've escaped their own country to a neighbouring country they've achieved their objective haven't they? They're safe.

Take Somalian's for example. Once they've made it to neighbouring Kenya or Ethiopia they're safe. So why do they then feel the need to travel all the way across Africa and through another half a dozen countries in Europe and then camp out in squalor in France for six months whilst trying to smuggle into the UK to be safe? There's no need. Because they were safe in Kenya or Ethiopia. And the reason they come - and will *keep on coming* - is because we are far too soft, or rather *our government* is far too soft, and they know we'll let them in. And until we *stop letting them in* they'll keep on coming, in droves.

If you feed a stray dog it'll keep coming back. Stop feeding it and it'll stop coming.

This country is turning into a right shit hole. There are towns and cities here that are more reminiscent of third world countries than they are of England. And as for those hypocritical halfwits that stand there waving their placards with 'Refugees Welcome' written on them at demonstrations, what I suggest is to take around two thousand asylum seekers and illegal immigrants and dump them in *their* town. Put them on *their* street. Put them in the houses next door to *them*. Put them in the houses opposite them. Put them in the flats above and below them. Have them hang around the street corners on *their* high street. Have them drive around *their* streets in clapped out transit vans (that probably aren't even insured) early in the morning pinching all the charity clothing bags. And then every Saturday and Sunday allow them all to gather in gangs in *their* city centre in pockets of Somalians, Afghans, Eastern Europeans, etc, making shoppers and families feel very uneasy - uneasy in their own country - and see how *they* like it (and stick a few hundred on Gary Lineker's street.) And if you *did do that* you can guarantee that at the next demonstration those idiots will have added the word 'NOT' on their placards in-between the words Refugees and Welcome.

You don't see it as much now because the camps in Calais have gone. But those 'poor' 18 - 25 year old males who have 'fled' their country claiming they are scared for their lives living there and have fled for fear of being attacked, or to escape the fighting weren't scared to attack British lorry drivers like they did were they when trying to hide in the back of their lorries? Neither are they scared to have pitch battles with the French police. And they also have no fear of fighting each other with knives and machetes in gang feuds in the camps like it's been shown on television they do. And so if they're capable of doing things like that then they are more than capable of fending for themselves in their own country.

I once read an article in the newspaper and in it a Labour MP said how immigration "painted a delightful picture of multicultural Britain." Delightful? What planet is he on? It might be delightful where *he* lives but it's certainly not delightful for a lot of people in many towns and cities across the UK. Including *my* town.

Maybe that MP should move to one district in Sheffield not far from where I live where it's overrun with Romanian Gypsies and which has been described as a "time bomb waiting to explode" by the local press and see if it's delightful to live there. As he'll soon discover, and as residents there know, it's *far* from delightful. Or perhaps he could go and live in a part of Oldham for a week or two that was in the papers not so long ago and see how delightful it is to live there. But then again he wouldn't *be able* to live there because as everyone knows it's a no-go area unless you're of a 'particular' ethnicity.

This 'delightful' country is going down the pan. It's an absolute joke. Only the joke isn't funny anymore and no-one's laughing. Well, apart from the refugees, asylum seekers and the illegal immigrants who come here that is. They think it's absolutely hilarious and they're laughing like hyenas. At us.

I often do daft things on the spur of the moment, and this one is about another daft thing that I once did on the spur of the moment and it gave my window cleaner the shock of his life.

A pal of mine, Colin, was a window cleaner and he used to do my windows for me, and I was in bed one Saturday morning having a bit of a lie-in when I heard some ladders being put up against the window. I knew straight away that it'd be Colin because he used to do the windows on our street every three weeks on a Saturday.

The window was open but the curtains were still closed. So I got out of bed, got a chair and put it in front of the window and stood on it, naked!

I sleep in the nude like a *lot* of people do. I also stand naked on chairs waiting to surprise their window cleaner like a lot of people *don't* do!

I could see the outline of him through the curtains as he came up the ladder and I waited until he was right at the top, directly in front of me. Then, as he started to clean the window, I grabbed the curtains and flung them wide open and stood there waving at him!

He nearly fell off his ladder. And *I* nearly fell off the chair. Because it wasn't Colin!

I didn't know that Colin was on holiday that week and that he'd got another window cleaner to do his round for him! I'd never seen this bloke before either. And judging by the look on the bloke's face he'd never seen a naked man before. Well he certainly hadn't seen one 20ft up a ladder standing on a chair in front of him waving at him with a big cheesy grin on his face!

He was just staring at me, open mouthed, clinging on to his ladders, thinking, "Who the fucking hell is this weirdo!" But rather than trying to explain myself and laugh it off and say, "Oh, sorry mate, I thought you were Colin," I just carried on standing there smiling at him. Then without batting an eyelid, I said, "Morning! Nice day for it."

He must have thought, "Nice day for it? Nice day for what? Cleaning windows or indecently exposing yourself!"

He didn't say a word. He was stunned. He just kept staring at me. So I said, "Do you fancy a cup of tea? I'll pop the kettle on," and put my thumb up at him and got off the chair and calmly walked out of the bedroom!

He was down the ladders like a shot! He didn't even bother cleaning the rest of my windows. He grabbed his ladders and was gone!

Colin thought it was hilarious when I told him what I'd done. And he told me another funny story about something that happened on another occasion when a different mate of his did his round for him while he was away.

He used to clean the windows at an old folks home that provided sheltered housing for pensioners. And when he got back from his holiday he got a right bollocking off the manager for letting a 'half wit' do the windows whilst he was away.

It was the middle of February and it was freezing cold and Colin said that it was absolutely bitter, and the forecast wasn't much better, so he decided to go to Tenerife for a week to get a bit of sun and he got his mate to cover for him. And before he went away he took his mate to the old folk's home to introduce him to the manager so the manager would know who he was when he turned up. I'm not quite sure why he needed to do that because it'd be fairly fucking obvious who he was when he turned up considering he'd be holding a bucket, a Chamois leather, a squeegee and a pair of 15ft aluminium ladders! But he introduced him anyway. And the manager asked Colin's mate that when he came would he mind trying to open the window of one of the flats that'd become stuck. He showed him the window, which was on the 2nd floor, and said that for some reason in the past someone had siliconed around the opener on the outside and the old lady who'd recently moved into the flat couldn't open it, and so Colin's mate said he'd sort it and said that the silicone probably just needed cutting off.

On the day, Colin's mate turned up at the old folk's home and got the ladders off the roof of his car and put them up against the window that was stuck on the second floor. And because it was brass monkey weather he put a pair of gloves on to keep his hands warm, which is a sensible thing to do when it's minus ten outside. But he also did a *not so* sensible thing.

Because it was bitterly cold, in order to keep his face and ears warm he put a ski mask on, a black one, the sort that bank robbers wear with the eyes and mouth cut out. It's also the sort that burglars, thugs and rapists wear, which, when you're working at an old people's home probably isn't the best thing to put on! He then got a couple of tools out of the van that he thought would come in handy to prise the window open. Those tools being a hammer, a chisel and a Stanley knife. And when he'd got them he started to climb the ladders.

Now imagine that you're the little old lady whose flat it was and that you're sat there watching television. And as you're sat there watching it you see a pair of ladders being put up against the window and some bloke wearing a balaclava and holding a hammer, a chisel and a Stanley knife climbs up it and starts trying to prise the window open. Do you think you'd be a little bit scared? Well the poor old lady who lived in the flat saw just that and she was absolutely terrified and she started screaming the place down! And thinking she was about to be burgled - or worse - pressed her panic button. And all hell broke loose!

Colin said he couldn't believe that anyone could be so stupid. He said that his mate could've given the old lady a heart attack. And if she wore a colostomy bag I bet she very nearly filled that too!

It can't be much fun getting old though can it? I remember calling at my Grandad's house once to see how he was and he said to me, "Every morning at seven o'clock I always have a piss, and at eight o'clock, without fail, I always have a crap." So I said to him, "Well what's wrong with that? Most people do." And he said, "Yeah, but I don't wake up 'til nine!"

Imagine looking out of your front window one morning and you see a man walking past who stops and picks up some litter from outside your house and then carry's on walking taking the litter with him. You'd probably think, "That was a good thing to do," Keep Britain Tidy, and all that! But if that man was to pick up that litter and then lean over your garden wall and open your bin and put it in it what would you think? You wouldn't think, "That was a good thing to do," would you? More than likely you'd think, "You cheeky bastard. Putting shit in my bin!" And you'd probably go out and say as much to him. And that's exactly what Robert - who I met in prison - did.

The only slight difference was that Robert was sat in his car about to go to work when he saw a guy, who was about the same age as him, late thirties, walk past and pick up a crisp packet and a paper cup that was on the floor outside his gate.

It annoyed Robert that the guy had put the rubbish, which wasn't his, in his bin so he got out of his car and said to the guy, "Oi, what do you think you're doing?"

The guy replied that he was just picking up some litter, trying to keep the street tidy, and Robert said, "Well don't put it in my bin."

The guy told Robert that it was only a crisp packet and a paper cup and that it was hardly going to fill his bin up, and Robert told the guy that he didn't care what it was he didn't want it in his bin. And he told the guy to take it out. The guy said no and an argument started. Robert then walked over to his bin and took the crisp packet and paper cup out of it and then walked over to the bloke and shoved them in the bloke's chest and told him to put them in his own bin.

The bloke told Robert that he was "pathetic" and he threw the crisp packet and cup back at him which infuriated Robert and he hit the guy. And the guy fell backwards, banged his head on the pavement and was knocked unconscious.

Immediately, Robert regretted what he'd done and he went from feeling angry to being concerned. And he phoned for an ambulance. But unfortunately, more so for the bloke, the damage had been done. The bloke never regained consciousness. And two days later he died from a blood clot on his brain.

Robert was then arrested, charged with manslaughter and six months later, after pleading guilty to involuntary manslaughter, he was sentenced to four years in prison.

Robert was married with a young daughter. The guy was also married with three young kids. And two families were left devastated.

It was totally out of character for Robert to do such a thing. It really was just a 'moment of madness', though it was more a moment of rage than a moment of madness.

It's no excuse for what he did, but it didn't help matters that Robert had been going through a bit of a tough time both at home and at work in the weeks and months prior to it happening. Money was tight. He was in debt. He was behind on his mortgage repayments and was worried that his house might be repossessed. There was talk of redundancies at work. His marriage was going through a bit of a rocky patch. And on that morning he'd had a row with his wife.

That aside, his actions show how people interpret things and how our emotions, and reactions, can be the exact opposite of each other in identical situations.

When Robert saw that bloke pick up that litter from outside his house he initially thought "that's a decent thing to do." But within a split second he viewed the situation totally different. A split second that shattered the lives of two families.

I was an estate agent for over forty years based in the south Manchester area and during my time in the business I saw some very peculiar things indeed in people's houses.

I had a viewing one day on a house and the buyers, who were a young couple, were restricted to the times they were available because of the hours and shifts they worked. I arranged a day and time that suited them and when I rang the gentleman whose house it was we were selling he said that he wouldn't be available that day and asked would I show them around. We had a set of keys and so I said that would be fine.

It was a pavement fronted terraced house, the type that when you opened the front door you stepped straight into the front room. On the day, which was around a week later, I met the couple outside, and when I opened the front door and walked in I saw – and so did the couple who were viewing the house – the gentleman asleep in the armchair. He was naked from the waist down and there was a box of tissues on the arm of the chair. There were also some screwed up tissues on top of the box. He also had his penis in his hand. The television was on too. And when we looked at it we saw a porn movie playing!

He must have fallen asleep after masturbating!

I didn't quite know what to say so I just said, "I think we best leave, quietly!" And we did. And when I got back to the office I rang the gentleman and told him that unfortunately the couple had had to cancel the viewing, and he said, "Oh, I forgot they were coming today." I thought, "Yes, I know you did!"

The couple did arrange a second viewing, which was actually their first, and a sale was agreed.

It's not the only time I've seen someone sat naked in their armchair. I also came across another gentleman who was sat naked in his armchair, though he wasn't asleep. He was wide awake. He was also playing a harmonica! It was funny, but sad at the same time. I went to his house to value it after being asked to do so by his daughter who said that they had to sell it because her dad was going into a care home. He had dementia and when she opened the front door I could hear a mouth organ being played. It was coming from the back room and his daughter said it was her dad who was playing it, or attempting to play it. She had no idea he was naked and when we walked in the room she said, "Oh god! Not again!"

He'd taken all of his clothes off and put them in a pile in the middle of the room. He hadn't just flung them on the floor, he'd folded them neatly in the order he'd taken them off, with his underpants on the top. And he was just sat their blowing away on his mouth organ! Obviously I didn't laugh, even though it was a funny sight. Though it is really sad how some people end up. It's sad how some people live too. I've been in many houses - a lot of which were rentals where the tenant had been evicted - and been lost for words when I've seen the squalor they've been living in. You feel sorry for some of them but you're also left feeling utterly disgusted by others, and one in particular springs to mind. And what makes this one even more disgusting is that the family, which consisted of the mum, her partner, three young toddlers and a fifteen month old baby, had only moved out, or rather been kicked out, only four days previously.

You'll have seen programmes on television about bad tenants and how when the landlord has evicted them they find that their house been wrecked and left uninhabitable. Well this was one such house. It was a pigsty. In fact, if a pig was to have walked into it it'd have walked straight back out again. It was filthy. Disgusting. It was an absolute hovel. A homeless person wouldn't have wanted to live in it. Honestly, it was that bad. Picture the worst house you've seen on one of those television programmes and then multiply it by a hundred and that'll give you an idea of what it was like. But what was utterly repulsive was that they'd been using the bath as a toilet. The toilet was blocked and there was faeces floating on the top. Faeces was also all over the bathroom floor, and the floor was soaking wet with urine. And so because the toilet was blocked they'd used the bath instead. That too was overflowing. It was full to the top with pee and excrement and there were dirty nappies floating on top of it all. And to think that only four days before three young children and a baby were living there.

Some people really shouldn't be allowed kids.

Another house I sold that had been rented out was left in the complete opposite state. It was immaculate. In fact, it was exactly the same as it was the first day the tenant moved in. Though six months later it transpired that he hadn't moved in at all. He'd just rented it out to carry out an elaborate scam ripping off BT. The guy was Asian. He was of smart appearance and very polite, and when he viewed the property he asked would it be okay to add a telephone point so I told him that it already had one in the hallway. And so he said would it be okay to add one in the front room. And I said that it wouldn't be a problem. And when I went back after he'd 'moved out' I saw that he had added one to the front room. He'd also added four in the back room. Three in the kitchen. And six in the front bedroom!

It turned out that not only was he smart in appearance he was also smart at scamming!

The office later got a call from the police's serious organised crime unit and they said that the guy was part of a crime syndicate and his gang had hacked into British Telecom's phone system, and other big organisations telephone systems, and rented out dozens of properties and put multiple telephone points in them. He said they mainly rented out properties in areas where a lot of Asian / Indian people lived and they were charging people £5 a week to use the telephones as often as they wanted. People were calling all over the world – for a fiver! It was well before mobile phones were as popular as they are and for £5 a week it was a bargain. The gang made hundreds of thousands of pounds from the scam and cost companies like BT £millions.

A woman also rented out a property for 'business purposes' as opposed to renting it out to live in. And her business was prostitution! She used the house as a brothel and she was rumbled after the neighbours became suspicious when they saw a steady stream of men and different girls going into the house on a daily basis. I also regularly came across houses that had been rented out and turned into cannabis factories. I was quite surprised actually at just how many people were doing it. Though after talking to the police (we had to inform them if we found that properties were being used for drugs) they said it was very common and that it was one of their biggest problems.

Though quite a few tenants weren't only growing cannabis they were using properties to hide much harder drugs like cocaine and heroin. And one person left his drugs in the house, which the police didn't find, when he was arrested. He was sentenced to eighteen months in prison and when he was released he came back for them. And it was a terrifying experience for the family who were living in it when he did.

A young woman and her boyfriend were living in the house with their three year old son. The house had a cellar and at around nine o'clock one evening there was a knock on the door and when the boyfriend opened it three men wearing balaclavas burst in. One had a gun and the other two were carrying machetes and a sledgehammer, and the one with the gun pointed it at the boyfriend and grabbed him by his neck and forced him into the living room where his girlfriend was sat watching television. Fortunately their son was upstairs in bed.

They were both absolutely petrified and when the boyfriend asked what the men wanted the one with the gun said, "Just sit down and don't speak." The one with the gun stayed in the living room with the couple and the one with the sledgehammer and the one holding the machete went into the cellar. The couple said they heard loud banging and smashing, and a couple of minutes later the two of them came back holding several large packets of white powder. The one with the gun told the couple not to ring the police and they calmly walked out of the house and got into a waiting car and drove off. The couple did as they were told to do and didn't ring the police but when they came in the office the next day and told us what had happened, *we* did.

I met the police at the house, and rather nonchalantly one of them said that it would've been the guy who was living there before who'd just been released from prison and had come back for his drugs. They must have searched the house in a similar nonchalant manner when they arrested him eighteen months previously. Perhaps if they'd have been more thorough they'd have found the drugs and prevented the couple from going through such a terrifying ordeal.

Though some tenants don't bother hiding their drugs, they just leave them on the kitchen worktop – chopped into lines ready to snort! They even offer you some!

I went into one rental property to carry out a periodic inspection and when I went in, the tenant, who was a 'young professional' type guy in his late twenties who worked in the city asked if I'd like a cup of tea. So I said yes. And I said to him that I'd have a quick look upstairs. And when I came back down after checking the bathroom and bedrooms he was stood with a rolled up twenty pound note in his hand with three lines of cocaine in front of him on the kitchen work surface! And he looked at me and said, "You don't mind do you?!"

The house was spotless. He'd looked after it and treated it as if it was his own, and he was a good tenant. Ordinarily, according to our rules, I would have had to have noted it but I just turned a blind eye to it. He even asked me if I "wanted a line!" So I said, "No thanks. A cup of tea will be fine!" Thankfully he didn't mistake the cocaine for sugar and put two spoonfuls in!

I was also once mistaken for a paedophile. It was around seven years ago. I went to value a house for a gentleman who'd contacted the office saying that he wanted to sell and that he wanted a quick sale, and when he opened the front door I had to do a double take – he looked just like me! I thought I was looking in a mirror at first! He thought the same thing and he laughed and said that we could pass for twins. I did what I had to do, took photographs, measured up and so on and then I sat down with him and discussed the selling price with him. He was happy with the price I gave him in order to achieve a quick sale, and making small talk more than anything, I asked him why he wanted to sell it quickly. And he said that the company he worked for were relocating over seventy miles away and that it was too far to travel every day. It seemed a plausible reason. However that wasn't the *real* reason why he wanted a quick sale.

I told him that I'd get the contract ready and said that I'd ring him to arrange a time for him to come into the office and sign it. And I got up, shook his hand and we walked into the hallway. I was in front of him and when I got to the front door I opened it and stood in the porch were four guys, two of whom were holding mobile phones up, pointing them at me. They were videoing me and one of them said to me, "Can you explain why you arranged to meet a fourteen year old girl for sex?"

They were a paedophile hunter group.

I was stunned - as anybody would be if someone accused them of being a paedophile. I wasn't quite sure what to say. So I said, "Sorry? What on earth are you talking about?" Then one of the other's said, "It's not him. It's the one behind." I turned around and looked at him and he looked as stunned as I did. He also looked rather sheepish. Well, not so much sheepish, he looked more ashamed. I then said to the four guys, "Can you let me past please. And can you make sure you delete that part of the video." And the one who spoke first said, "Don't worry. We will. We'll also be passing it on to the police."

As well as being mistaken for a paedophile I've also been referred to as a male stripper! A lady had been in the office and asked could we value her house for her as she was thinking of selling. She was going on holiday to Ibiza the following day for two weeks with her friends so I made an appointment for the week she was back. And similar to the gentleman who was sat in his armchair asleep half naked with a porn movie playing on his television who'd forgotten I was coming, this lady forgot I was coming too.

When I went I knocked on the front door and a woman who I'd never seen before answered it. She was holding a glass of red wine and she looked at me and shouted back over her shoulder, "The male stripper's arrived girls!" I then heard another woman's voice shout back, "Get him in here!" I then heard lots of women laughing.

A few seconds later the lady whose house it was appeared and when she saw me she said the same thing that the gentleman who fell asleep watching a porno" said, which was, "Oh, I forgot you were coming today!" So I went in and when I walked in the front room there was about fifteen women sat there - ever so slightly intoxicated - who all cheered and started chanting "Get 'em off!" I glanced around the room and on top of the dining table there were sex aids, vibrators, rampant rabbits and sexy women's underwear and lingerie - I walked straight into an Ann Summers party!

Take my word for it, there's nothing worse than being the only male in a room full of drunken women! I was lucky to get out alive! I've also been lucky to have done the job I've been doing for the last forty years. I've seen it all.

There can't be many jobs were you're mistaken for a paedophile one week and mistaken for a male stripper the next - and get to watch porn inbetween!

As you probably remember, before DVD players were around everything was on video and one day I received a video cassette tape in the post. It didn't have a note or anything with it saying who it was from it was just the tape. It wasn't even in a case and when I looked at it I could see by the reels that the tape was halfway through and not at the beginning. So I put it on. And I took it straight off again. That's because as soon as it began playing I saw that it was a hardcore gay porn movie!

It may well have made the ideal film for a movie night for some but it wasn't the kind of film I'd settle down to if I was having a night in! Someone, more than likely a mate, had sent it to me for a bit of a giggle. So I thought I'd do the same thing and pass it on to someone else. And it worked out better than I thought!

By pure coincidence I'd just recorded a documentary that was on television the week before about Eric Cantona. I'd recorded it for a mate of mine who was a big Man United fan and his favourite player was Cantona. But instead of giving him the tape that I'd recorded for him I gave him the gay porn one, and on the label I wrote 'Eric Cantona documentary'.

When I went around to his flat and gave it him he was dead chuffed and he said, "That's brilliant. Thanks for recording it for me. I missed it the other as I was at the match." So I told him that I thought he might have been at Old Trafford for the game and that's why I recorded it for him. He then said, "Oh Bollocks!" so I said, "What?" and he said, "My video recorder is knackered!" But then he said, "Ah! I know. My Mum and Dad have got a video player. I'll take it round there and watch it." So I said, "Yeah, that's a great idea. I'm sure they'll enjoy it!"

His mum and dad were very straight laced. They went to church every Sunday. They didn't drink. They didn't smoke. And they didn't swear. And they didn't watch porn either. And they certainly didn't watch GAY porn! But they did like football. And they too followed Manchester United like my mate did.

Two days later I was sat at home watching the tele" and the phone rang so I picked it up and it was my mate and he said, "You cunt!!" So I started laughing and said, "You've watched the video then?" and he said, "Yes, I did watch it. And so did my fucking Mum and Dad!"

He said that he went around to his mum and dad's and he asked them did they fancy watching a documentary about Eric Cantona and they both said yes. So he gave the video to his mum to put on whilst he went to get a glass of water from the kitchen. And he said that as he took a sip of it he heard a man's voice coming from the living room say, "Which one of you two wants my cock first?"

He said his first thoughts were "I hope that's not my Dad asking me and my mum that question!" And then he thought, "And I can't see it being a scene from the documentary either where Eric Cantona is in the showers after a match asking the Neville brothers that question!" And he soon realised that it *wasn't* his dad or King Eric that had said it when the man's voice was immediately followed by his mum shouting "What the bloody hell is this you've brought around!"

He said that he coughed and spat the water everywhere, then dropped the glass and shot into the living room. And when he looked at the television he saw three naked men, two of which were on all fours on a bed with their bollocks hanging down and pulling their arse cheeks apart and the third one was stood behind them with a massive hard on!

He said he ran across the room and dived across the carpet and pressed the eject button on the video player and when he took it out he looked at his dad and his dad was just sat there open mouthed looking totally shell shocked at what he'd just seen. He said the expression on his dad's face reminded him of the scene from Father Ted where Ted kicks Bishop Brennan up the arse and Bishop Brennan goes into a trance like state not quite believing Ted has had the audacity to do it him - and Rob's dad had gone into a similar trance!

Being an avid Manchester United fan my mate had seen Eric Cantona put in some marvellous performances over the years but I don't think he was quite expecting to see a performance like that! His mum and dad definitely weren't that's for sure!

The Puss In Boots pub that I talked about earlier was one of the best pubs around at the time. It's still there now though it's more of a family type pub these days that focuses more on food. They do a nice carvery there on a Sunday and I went there not so long ago with my wife and kids. It was nice in there. It was also nice to go in there and leave in one piece as opposed to leaving there covered in blood after being battered senseless with a metal cosh like what used to happen whenever I went in there!

Everyone who's anyone used to go to the Puss' back in the day. It was the place to be. The place to be if you wanted to get a fucking good hiding!

John Fury, Tyson Fury's dad, used to go in there. He used to stand and have a chat whenever he came in, mainly with Tony who was working on the door. They used to talk about boxing as John Fury was a boxer like Tony was. Tyson Fury would only have been around 16 or 17 years old at the time but I remember John Fury saying, "Mark my words. My son will be world champion one day."

He had good foresight didn't he.

And Tyson Fury is arguably one of the best world champions ever. Even more so considering the setbacks/mental health issues he's had etc. And to come back and retain his titles the way he has done is a magnificent achievement. Possibly the most magnificent ever.

Another boxer, or ex-boxer, that used to come in was Billy Isaacs. He knew Tony from his boxing days and he'd come in and see him every now and then. Billy was extremely well known - and extremely feared - not only around the Manchester/Stockport area where he was from but in London too. He really was a fearsome figure. He was around 6ft 4in and weighed around 19st and he had a shaved head with tear-drop tattoos under his left eye which made him look *even more* intimidating!

A tear-drop tattoo under the eye originated in Mexico and is associated with gang or prison culture and can signify different things. It can either represent that you've served a lengthy prison sentence or that you've committed murder or that you've lost someone close to you in a gangland killing. I'm not quite sure why Billy had one (I think he had three actually) under his eye though he was once cleared of murder. And he'd also served time in prison. Although in America and in South American countries a tear-drop under the eye also indicates that the person has been raped in prison. Though I fucking doubt very much that happened to Billy in Strangeways and *that's* what his tear-drop signified!

Billy died in 2013 after a freak accident at his home in Ireland where he'd moved too. There was speculation and rumours at the time that because of his past and his involvement in the underworld he'd been 'bumped off' but the rumours turned out to be false after it was revealed that he'd died after he'd climbed onto a wheelie bin in order to get through an open ground floor window after he'd locked himself out of his house and slipped and fell inwards through the window and landed awkwardly on his head and neck which resulted in him dying from 'positional asphyxia'.

He was discovered the following day by a builder who he'd arranged to meet at his house. It was a sad end really for someone who was once tipped by many in the boxing world when he first began his boxing career to be one of Britain's top professionals.

He was very similar to Chris (Little) in that he was involved in the same world that Chris was involved in. He was a big handy lad like Chris, he was an ex-pro boxer like Chris was and he was feared like Chris was too. However they weren't particularly keen on each other. I remember one night when Billy came in the Puss and Boots and when he was talking to Tony he started slagging Chris off. It was about four years after Chris had been shot and Billy must have forgotten that Chris was a pal of mine and Tony's, and so Tony said to him that he knew he had his differences with Chris but at the end of the day Chris was a mate of ours and said so whatever opinions he had of Chris to maybe keep them to himself.

Tony didn't say it in a nasty or aggressive manner he was just politely reminding him. And fair play to Billy he said, "No, you're right. I shouldn't be slagging him off when he's not here to defend himself. And I shouldn't be slagging him off to his mates either." And he apologised.

I never did know what the underlying problem between Chris and Billy was. A clash of personalities/conflicting personalities is probably the wrong term to use to describe the problem they had because their personalities were pretty much the same and didn't really conflict. It was probably more of a case of 'this town ain't big enough for the both of us' kind of thing. And in the end it was Billy that left. Though he didn't leave due to the animosity between him and Chris. He left to pursue his career as a professional boxer. Though not long before he left, him and Chris had a run in at the Fir Tree pub. And there were two different stories going around as to what the outcome was. I didn't see it happen, I only know what Chris told me and what the landlord of the Fir Tree told me the following night when I went in as he said he saw it.

It was a Thursday night if I remember rightly and Chris was working on the door on his own like he usually did on a Thursday and Billy turned up. Chris said he was stood in the foyer talking to Billy and things got a bit heated and he chinned Billy knocking him to the floor. He didn't knock him out and he said Billy got up and backed away down the steps into the car park and said to Chris, "That's not the fucking end of it," and left. The landlord said that's how it had happened as well and said that he saw it from where he was standing behind the bar. Although another story started going around that Billy had chinned Chris.

Not long afterwards, Billy went to live in London where he turned professional boxer. His manager was Gary Mason, the former British Heavyweight champion and I always remember an interview Billy did when he first turned pro' during which he said that a good night out for him would be to have eight pints, a curry and a fight!

You can take the lad out of Stockport but you can never take Stockport out of the lad!

A bit like Chris's professional boxing career, Billy's didn't last long either and after retiring from professional boxing he took a different career path, the same path Chris took. And he became known as a 'gangland enforcer' and worked for some of the most dangerous and well known crime families in London. He also worked for Dave Courtney. I think Dave said Billy lived at his house, 'Camelot Castle' for three years too.

I've been to Dave's house a couple of times myself though I didn't stay for three years like Billy did. I think Dave had had enough of me after three hours! I went after he'd asked me to help him write a book he was thinking of doing. And so I put a few chapters together for him and sent them to him. But nothing came of it as he had a heart attack and had to put the book on hold. He must have read what I'd written, thought, "Fuck me! What have I asked this daft cunt to write my book for me for!" and collapsed to the floor clutching his chest!

Sadly, Dave is no longer with us. He took his own life not so long ago as you probably know. Dave wasn't a 'mate' of mine. I only knew him because of my books. But when you spoke to him he made you *feel like a mate.* He was warm and friendly and if he could help you - like a mate would - he would. He actually wrote the foreword for my book Hardmen Gangsters Jokers and Pranksters which was nice of him to do.

I'm not a hardman *or* a gangster by the way. I just knew one or two. Though not quite as many as Dave did! Joker and prankster on the other hand, I was right at the top of the tree for that! I've done some right idiotic things. As you've probably surmised!

I first met Dave after I'd written the book I mentioned earlier, Gym'll Fix It. I was still into bodybuilding when I wrote it and it was about getting into shape and dieting. It also contained warped humour and sick jokes about

Jimmy Savile. Hence the title! And when Dave read it he found it funny. Though he obviously took no notice of the diet advice that was in it!

About fifteen years previously I'd read Dave's book 'Stop The Ride' and as I was nearing finishing Gym'll Fix It I saw it in WH Smith's one day and I remembered how good, and how funny, it was. And I thought, "That'll come in handy to help 'polish' mine." So I nicked a copy of it! Well Dave does say in it, "If it's not nailed down, pinch it." So I did! And when I got half way though it there were about a dozen things in it that I'd put in mine, some of them more or less word for word. And bearing in mind Dave had written it in 1999, and that's when I'd first read it, those things couldn't have been in my subconscious for all of that time. One or two maybe but not a dozen! There was even a snake called 'Fang' in his and I'd called a dog in mine Fang as well! And I thought, "Fucking hell! If Dave Courtney reads my book he'll think I've copied half of his!" So I re-worded a few of the stories I'd written. Although there were one or two others in his book that when I read them I thought, "Hmmm, I like that one," and "Oh, that's a funny one! I'll just 'borrow' those and change them slightly. I'm sure Dave won't mind. He seems like a nice bloke!"

And it turned out that he *didn't* mind. And that he *was* a nice bloke. And the stories and one liner's I nicked off him fitted in my book very nicely!

It was purely coincidence that I'd written virtually identical things to what Dave had done and I don't think it was a case of great minds thinking alike but more a case of *silly* minds thinking alike! As a matter of fact a few years later in an interview Dave did with the Manchester Evening News after he'd asked me to write his book for him he said to the reporter, "Nick's books are the closest you'll get to mine." And considering he's had several bestsellers and sold millions of copies worldwide I took that as a massive compliment. It was also a really nice thing of him to say. Mind you, my books *would be* the closest thing you'd get to his because I've pinched half the fucking things in mine from his!

Chances are, Dave would never have read my book and he'd have been none the wiser to the things in it. But out of courtesy, and to avoid being sued for breach of copyright - and avoid being smashed in the face off him with a knuckleduster! - I sent him a copy when I'd finished it explaining everything, and not long after we met. And he came out with a funny one liner when we met too.

I was in Shepperton in Surrey at the time and I'd arranged to meet him at his house and rather than drive because I thought that I'd probably end up having a drink with him, which I did, I got the train. And as I was on the way to Waterloo station in London Dave rang and said there'd been a slight change of plan and could I meet him at a place called The Prince George's Club in Raynes Park as he had to meet someone there and so I said okay.

It was a private members club and Dave said to tell them that it was him I was meeting there and they'd let me in, and he said that he was on his way and that he'd be about an hour. As luck would have it Raynes Park was on the way to Waterloo and it was the next stop but one so I got off and made my way to the club and when I walked up to the doors I saw that entry was via the intercom and so I pressed the buzzer and this bloke said, "Yes, can I help you."

I've never been one to 'drop names.' Not that I *was* dropping Dave's name. And it wasn't the kind of name dropping like I mentioned earlier in the book. But even though he'd said to tell them it was him I was meeting I felt a little bit uncomfortable/awkward, if you know what I mean, saying, "I'm here to meet Dave Courtney." Some of you will know where I'm coming from I'm sure. And some of you will probably think I'm a tit-head! But, that's me. So I just said, "I'm here to meet someone," and the bloke pressed the buzzer and opened the door.

Those of you who know me will know that I wear shorts year round. Whatever the weather, be it sunny, pissing down, minus ten or knee deep in snow, I'll have shorts on. Funerals and court appearances are probably the only exceptions. Thankfully the latter aren't as frequent as they once were! (Though I may well have one pending thanks to that stuck up old cow from Hale who complained about the flyer.) Funerals on the other hand, well, the older you get the more frequent they seem to become.

When I went in and opened the next door that lead into the lounge area I saw that there were about twenty or so people sat around talking and drinking and when I walked in they all *stopped* talking and drinking and looked at me.

You'll have seen the old western films where the gunslinger or a stranger pushes the swinging wooden saloon doors open and walks into the bar and the piano player stops playing and everyone stops what they're doing and stares at him, and that's how *I* felt! It was a bit of a chilly day too and they were all looking at me as if to say, "Who's this daft bastard in Lonsdale shorts!"

I felt a right cunt stood there with everyone staring at me and the first thing that crossed my mind was that when I opened my mouth and spoke and they heard my Manchester accent they'd think, "Who's this daft *Northern bastard* in Lonsdale shorts!!"

The fella behind the bar said, "Did you say you were here to meet someone?" And just as I was about to reply I heard another voice say, "Are you Nick?" And when I looked over I saw a smartly dressed bloke who looked like he was in his mid sixties sat at the end of the bar. He looked vaguely familiar and so I said to him, "I am mate, yes." And he said to the fella behind the bar, "He's okay." And the bartender nodded, the piano player started playing again, and everyone stopped staring at me and began talking to each other again! And *I* didn't feel as much of a cunt!

The bloke was the person who Dave had arranged to meet and Dave had rang him and asked him to keep an eye out for me and he bought me a pint and we began chatting. He said, "Dave mentioned that you write books," and I said, "That's right, I do. And he said, "I've been in a book myself," and so I said, "Really? What book was that?" And he said, "Ultimate Hard Bastards by Kate Kray."

It was Ronnie Field. Who was part of the Kray's Firm.

I'd read the book which was why he looked vaguely familiar although the photo of him in the book was taken several years earlier. And he was a proper hard bastard too by all accounts. He was also a really nice bloke. Just like Dave was. He said he ran the club and he showed me around it. The club had an upstairs level to it where they had a couple of snooker tables and he asked me if I played. I told him that I used to do and that I'd had a century break to which he said, "You were half decent then," which I suppose I was. (As Dave later found out!) And as we were coming back downstairs Dave came walking in with his girlfriend at the time (Debbie, I think she was called.) We shook hands and we stood at the bar with Ronnie and a couple of other people they knew chatting and having a bit of a laugh. And after a couple of rounds I said, "It's my round, I'll get them in," and Dave said, "No, *I'll* get them in," so I said, "No, I'll get them. It's my shout. You've already got them in once." But Dave again insisted that he get them. And again, I insisted that *I'd* get them! To which Dave said, "Look, you can't even afford a pair of long trousers y'cunt - or a decent pair of shorts - let alone get a fucking round in!" And everyone pissed themselves laughing at me!

And Dave got the round in!

But later that day the tables turned. On a *pool* table. And *I* ended up laughing at Dave.

After we left the club we went back to his house and we had a few games of pool. Dave was shit hot at pool. He also played with one hand which is an extremely difficult thing to do. I played snooker for many years and I certainly couldn't have done it as good as Dave did. However I did have a little bit of a trick shot that I could do. Dave had beaten me a couple of times already and when I broke off in the following game I potted two balls off the break. The balls had split nicely in my favour and a few shots later I was on the black which I just needed to pot to win. And when I got down to play it, once I'd eyed the shot up I looked at Dave, lifted one leg off the floor and stretched it out behind me, smiled at him, shut my eyes, turned my head away from the table and potted the black!

I think that must have been the only time that Dave has lost a game of pool to someone who was standing on one leg with his eyes closed whilst looking away from the table! And when I opened my eyes and stood up and looked at him, laughing, he said, "You fucking piss taking northern bastard!"

I also had a few photographs taken with him including the 'usual' holding guns pic", which, as I said to him I wasn't particularly bothered about having taken. But just like he insisted on getting the round in he said to have the photo taken as it would be good publicity for my books. And he was right.

Something else that made me laugh that day, albeit to myself, was when he first came in The Prince George's club.

He had white pants on, a white shirt and he had a long white coat too. And he was wearing sandals and he had a pair of sunglasses on his head. And when he walked in the lounge nobody battered an eyelid and I thought, "Fuck me. He walks in looking like Marty out of Randal and Hopkirk, on his holidays, and nobody gives him a second glance. But I walk in wearing Lonsdale shorts, a jumper and a pair of trainers and everyone stares at me like I've got two fucking heads!" (Marty was the ghost in Randal and Hopkirk, a television series in the 1970"s. If you've never heard of it look it up and you'll get the joke!)

But that's Dave for you, he carried things off better than your normal, average, everyday bloke and he led the life that was a million miles away from the normal average everyday bloke's life too. But even though his everyday life wasn't average or normal Dave himself was a normal everyday kinda' bloke. And even though he was who he was he didn't think he was better than anyone else and that's why he was liked by so many people. He led his life the way HE wanted to. And he ended his life the way he wanted to as well. The ride may well have come to an end for him but the memory will live on for a long time yet.

If you enjoyed this book you may enjoy our other books...

Three Vaginas And A Permanent Erection
Silly Facts, Silly Questions, and Silly Answers
By Asilic Unt

Did you know that you can tell the sex of a horse by counting its teeth? Although it's much easier to just look underneath and see if there's a massive cock swinging around!

Did you know that semen is ejaculated faster than Usain Bolt can run?

Did you know that a pigeon sees more frames per second than human beings do which gives them more time to asses danger and so only move if they have to. Which could explain why they leave it until the very last second before flying out of the way (causing you to think you've ran it over and squashed it) when you're driving towards one that's nonchalantly sat in the middle of the road!

And did you know that contrary to what many people believed there never were any characters called Seaman Staines, Master Bates, and Roger The Cabin Boy in the 1970's kids cartoon series Captain Pugwash. That said, in the Urban Dictionary, Pugwash is defined as "Cum that drains out of the anus after anal intercourse."

And to think we used to sit there eating our tea whilst we watched that as well!

If you enjoy watching the television programme 'QI' then chances are you'll enjoy this book. The only slight difference between this book and QI is that the questions, answers and facts that are in it are slightly sillier than those on the hit TV show. One or two are slightly more vulgar as well!

Nonetheless, they are very interesting. They're quite surprising too. And some are quite bemusing!

Another difference between this book and QI (which aren't connected in any way. We've been asked to point that out so the author doesn't get sued!) is that whereas the hosts and panelists of the television show are knowledgeable and intellectual people, the author isn't. He's a silly cunt! As you may have guessed from his name!

We've also been asked to point out that Asilic's mate doesn't really masturbate whilst driving his train at 125mph on the West Coast Mainline between Manchester Piccadilly and London Euston. Asilic just said that for a comparison of speeds. And no pigeons were ejaculated on either. They were too quick!

And despite what's being said in the pub where Asilic goes drinking the title isn't referring to Asilic and his wife! (It refers to Kangaroos and Alligators.) Though one of Asilic's mates did once sustain an erection for over nine hours. Not that he wanted too. But he didn't have much choice in the matter after being spiked with Viagra on his stag do! Although that particular incident did prove one fact to be right. And that's that it *is* possible for men to urinate when they've got a hard-on. Though not much of the piss goes where it's supposed to go – in the toilet. Most of it ends up running down the walls and dripping off the bathroom ceiling! On the plus side you do get to have a shower whilst having a slash!

Got a broad sense of humour? Like amusing funny facts? Then you'll like this book!

Well Isle Beef Hooked, I Own A Racehorse!

By Ivan R Don and Fannif Art

If you've come across this book and thought, "Well I don't particularly like horse racing so it'll be of no interest to me," hang on a minute. Because despite the title - and despite the fact that the original idea for the book by the person who first thought about writing it was for it to be about horse racing - it's got very little to do with the sport! What it actually has got is extraordinary true life stories by ordinary everyday people that range from the frightening to the fascinating and the wonderful and the weird, to the horrific and the hilarious and the heart-breaking and the inhumane.

Graham Patterson loved horse racing. He was an apprentice jockey when he was younger but he wasn't quite good enough and never got to fulfil his dream of becoming a professional jockey. But his passion for racing stayed with him. He loved it. He also dreamt of writing a book about the names of racehorses and the stories behind the naming of them. Sadly, he never got to fulfil that dream either because not long after he started writing the book he was given the news that he had terminal cancer and he died shortly afterwards. So Graham's mates came to the rescue to make his dream come true and wrote the book for him. Although it isn't quite what Graham had in mind! But, as Graham's wife said when she read it, Graham would've absolutely loved it. And if you've got a broad sense of humour - and aren't easily shocked - it's odds on you'll love it too!

The stories will have you crying, cringing, wincing, wailing, laughing (hysterically) and lost for words. And if you do like horse racing - and like a bet on the gee gees - there's a fantastic story at the end titled Jumping For Joy in which 'Ivan', one of the author's, tells of how thanks to Graham he won over £20,000 on an accumulator he placed. Ivan literally WAS jumping for joy. All around his living room with his betting slip slapped on his forehead! It's a 'racehorse' book like no other. One that well and truly deserves to be in the winner's enclosure. It's also one that both fans of horse racing and those who have no real interest in the 'sport of kings' will thoroughly enjoy.

Or should that be *thoroughbred* enjoy!

Laugh? I Nearly Shat Myself

By Ivan R Don and Fannif Art

If Carlsberg did adult humour books...

If you've read Ivan and Fanni's last book Well Isle Beef Hooked, I Own A Racehorse! you'll know that a number of the stories came courtesy of their pal Billy. And as you'd have gathered after reading Billy's stories - and as Ivan and Fanni put in the foreword of *this* book - Billy is a bit of a 'rum fucker.' In fact, he's A LOT of a rum fucker! And what Billy hasn't seen and done in his life isn't worth writing about. What he HAS seen and done in his life on the other hand IS worth writing about. So Ivan and Fanni got Billy to write it!

Whatever the situation, Billy tries to see the funny side. Though there are times - such as being fitted up by the police and finding out that one of your best mates is a paedophile - when even Billy found it hard to laugh. And being brought up by a strict domineering alcoholic dad, who later committed suicide, wasn't much fun for Billy either. Though Billy did see the funny side, and the irony, of being charged with the same offence as Ronnie Biggs and The Great Train Robbers and being sent to prison. The only slight difference was that when Ronnie and the proper train robbers opened the mail bags that they'd pinched and found they were stuffed with millions of pounds, when Billy and his mate opened the bags that they'd pinched they found that all they were stuffed with were old copies of Readers Digest!

It's one of the funniest books you'll ever read and the stories will have you in stitches laughing. And one or two people required stitches during the course of writing some of them! Including a cheating husband Billy knew who had his wedding tackle lobbed off by his wife whilst he was asleep in bed after she found out what he'd been up to. She used a pair of garden shears to cut them off with and when she was arrested she told police she was "quite surprised how easy they came off." Like Billy says, no doubt her husband was quite surprised too when he woke up and saw his wife standing by the bed with a pair of garden shears in one hand and his knackers in the other!

Everyone's idea of humour is different. But, as Billy puts;

"Whether we've got the same sense of humour or not, we're all just the same. And everyone I've mentioned in this book are no different from me or you; Gangsters, dodgy characters, bent coppers, nasty coppers, horrible Hollywood superstar action hero's (who like to kick their pet dogs half to death and knock seven bells out of their wife) well known celebrities and television personalities, footballers, piss taking taxi drivers, useless builders, builders who can't control their bowels and blokes on jolly boy's outings who have no control over their erections! We're all the same. Some of them may have more money than me and you, and some of them may be more famous than me and you. But they're no different from me and you - or any better. And if you stripped all the money and the fame and the celebrity status away and we all stripped naked and stood next to each other in a line it'd reveal what we all know: that all men are exactly the same. I'm exactly the same as you, and you are exactly the same as me. You've got two arms, two legs and a twelve inch cock just like I have.

Well two out of three ain't bad for you!"

The title says it all. And if Carlsberg did do adult humour books they'd definitely do one like this! As Billy's old pal Bernard Manning once said, "Don't take life too seriously. Have a laugh and a joke. Because if you don't you'll lead a very miserable life." And that's the attitude Billy takes. And you'll probably take the same attitude towards life too after you've read this book.

Not All Husbands Are Annoying - Some Are Dead

By Ruth Jennings

I remember WHERE I married my husband and I remember WHEN I married my husband. I just can't remember WHY I married him.

Three words that will shatter your husband's ego: Is it in?

What do toilets, birthdays and anniversaries have in common? Husbands miss them all.

A woman went to the doctors to get her husband's blood test results and the receptionist said to her, "We'll need a urine sample, a stool sample and a sample of your husband's semen." So the woman said, "I'll drop a pair of his underpants off tomorrow."

Ruth Jennings was happily married for ten years. Ten out of thirty isn't bad! She's now happily divorced and to celebrate she's released this book which is crammed full of jokes about husbands and marriage. And if you're married, or divorced like Ruth is, you'll find it absolutely hilarious. It'll also make an ideal gift for 'Hubby'. Though don't be surprised if your husband files for divorce after he's read it!

Can You Spare A Multi Millionaire A Pound Please

By Adam Gleeson

If a tramp asked you if you could spare him a cigarette and after you kindly gave him one he took £200 out of his pocket and gave it to you what would you think? Or if you saw a homeless man sat in a shop doorway and you gave him a bit of loose change and he got up and gave you a handful of £20 notes how would you react? And imagine just how elated you'd feel if you were up to your eye balls in debt and were about to be evicted from your home and a Good Samaritan came along and cleared your rent arrears for you and paid off all your debts and then paid for you and your two kids to go to Disney World in Florida. Well those scenarios - and dozens more like them - have actually happened. And the 'tramp' and the 'homeless man' and the Good Samaritan are one and the same person.

Whilst driving his car one day, Adam Gleeson pulled onto a pay and display car park and as he walked towards the machine to get a ticket he noticed a man sat in a Bentley Continental, a car that was worth around £150,000, parked in the bay next to the machine. And as Adam was getting his ticket the man got out of the Bentley and asked him could he spare him a £1 so he too could get a ticket. Adam started laughing and jokingly said to the man, "Are you taking the mickey!? You're driving a car like that and you're asking me for a pound!"

The man explained that he'd left his house without his wallet and didn't have any change for a ticket and so Adam thought well it's something we've all done, left the house without any money, and he gave the man a pound coin so he could get a car parking ticket. And the man thanked him. Put his hand in his pocket. Took two £50 notes out. Gave them to Adam - along with his £1 coin back - and got in his Bentley and drove off!

It transpired that Adam had just past one of Tom's - the driver of the Bentley - kindness tests that he sometimes does where he rewards people for showing kindness towards others. It also transpired that Tom was a multi-millionaire worth in excess of £100 million and who one day realised that he'd never get around to spending all the money he's got, so he started giving it away - to complete strangers in bizarre and unusual ways. Leaving them totally bewildered into the bargain!

From sending hundreds of pounds inside Christmas cards to people he's never met, to hiding wads of cash inside newspapers on the London Underground for people to find and leaving it hanging out of cash dispensers for people to take, to clearing a single mum's debts and paying for her and her two young daughters to go on a dream holiday to Disney World in Florida which totalled over £10,000, to taking another family he'd never met before out on his yacht for the day in Majorca and then paying for their holiday too, which amounted to over £5,000. He's also put a homeless man up in a hotel in Brighton for a week and thrown $100 dollar bills (the equivalent of a week's wage) out of his hotel window in Thailand to local Thai people on the street below! Tom also tells of why he once gave a woman in Tesco's a £100 because she sneezed, carried a nurse's shopping to her car for her and then gave her £250, bought an elderly couple an expensive plasma television in Curry's, how he goes into shops and hides money inside clothes and books for people to find when they buy them and take them home, why he paid for fifty people's MOT's at a garage, and how he asked a road sweeper if he believed in the saying 'where there's muck there's money' and then watched as he dived into his own litter bin after he told him he'd just thrown a thousand pounds in it!

He also once bought someone an ice cream in the Lake District. Along with the other forty people that were standing in the queue behind him!

Bizarre? Slightly Odd? Maybe. Does Tom's generosity brighten up people's day and put a smile on their faces? Definitely. And to Tom that's all that matters. And it's one of the most remarkable stories you'll ever read.

All of our books are available on Amazon

Printed in Great Britain
by Amazon